HARLEQUIN®
Presents™

Welcome to February's fabulous collection of books
from Harlequin Presents!

Be sure not to miss the final installment of the brilliant
series THE ROYAL HOUSE OF NIROLI. Will the beautiful
island of Niroli finally be able to crown the true
heir to the throne? Find out in *A Royal Bride at the
Sheikh's Command* by favorite author Penny Jordan!
Plus, continuing her trilogy about three passionate and
brooding men, THE RICH, THE RUTHLESS AND THE
REALLY HANDSOME, Lynne Graham brings you
The Greek Tycoon's Defiant Bride, where Leonidas is
determined to take the mother of his son as his wife!

Also this month…can a billionaire ever change his
bad-boy ways? Discover the answer in Miranda Lee's
The Guardian's Forbidden Mistress! Susan Stephens
brings you *Bought: One Island, One Bride,* where a
Greek tycoon seduces a feisty beauty, then buys her
body and soul. In *The Sicilian's Virgin Bride* by
Sarah Morgan, Rocco Castellani tracks down his
estranged wife—and will finally claim his virgin bride!
In *Expecting His Love-Child,* Carol Marinelli tells the
story of Millie, who is hiding a secret—she's pregnant
with Levander's baby! In *The Billionaire's Marriage
Mission* by Helen Brooks, it looks like wealthy Travis
Black won't get what ~~he wants for once~~—or will he?
Finally, new author Ch~~...~~
innocent virgin who ~~...~~
tycoon for one night ~~...~~
in her brilliant debu~~...~~
Happy reading!

Harlequin Presents®

ITALIAN
HUSBANDS

They're tall, dark…and ready to marry!

If you love reading about our sensual
Italian men, don't delay, look out for the
next story in this great miniseries!

Available only from Harlequin Presents®

Sarah Morgan

THE SICILIAN'S VIRGIN BRIDE

ITALIAN HUSBANDS

TORONTO • NEW YORK • LONDON
AMSTERDAM • PARIS • SYDNEY • HAMBURG
STOCKHOLM • ATHENS • TOKYO • MILAN • MADRID
PRAGUE • WARSAW • BUDAPEST • AUCKLAND

ISBN-13: 978-0-373-12703-0
ISBN-10:   0-373-12703-0

THE SICILIAN'S VIRGIN BRIDE

First North American Publication 2008.

www.eHarlequin.com

Printed in U.S.A.

All about the author...
Sarah Morgan

SARAH MORGAN was born in Wiltshire and started writing at the age of eight when she produced an autobiography of her hamster.

At the age of eighteen she traveled to London to train as a nurse in one of London's top teaching hospitals, and she describes those years as extremely happy and definitely censored! She worked in a number of areas in the hospital after she qualified.

Over time her writing interests moved on from hamsters to men, and she started creating romance fiction. Her first completed manuscript, written after the birth of her first child, was rejected by Harlequin, but the comments were encouraging, so she tried again. On the third attempt her manuscript *Worth the Risk* was accepted unchanged. She describes receiving the acceptance letter as one of the best moments of her life, after meeting her husband and having her two children.

Sarah still works part-time in a health-related industry and spends the rest of the time with her family, trying to squeeze in writing whenever she can. She is an enthusiastic skier and walker, and loves outdoor life.

CHAPTER ONE

SHE flew in at night, in a small private plane that she'd chartered using the last of her cash. The brim of her hat was pulled low over her eyes, concealing almost all of her features, and her hair was ruthlessly subdued and twisted out of sight. She wore a plain black coat over black trousers. No make-up. No jewellery. It was the outfit of a woman who didn't want to attract attention to herself. *The outfit of a woman who was hiding.*

Had the pilot looked closely he might have remarked on the ashen colour of her skin, or the slight shake of her hands as she clutched her one small bag. Had he looked closer still he might have seen the fire in her blue eyes and the determined jut of her chin. But he wasn't looking. He'd taken one brief glance at her as she'd boarded the plane and immediately lost interest. He'd been paid an enormous sum of money to do exactly that, but all the same Chessie sat rigid in her seat, unable to relax as she stared through the small window into the darkness. She'd refused the offer of refreshment with a brief shake of her head, unable to contemplate placing any further strain on her already churning stomach.

Any minute now they'd be landing in Sicily, and the thought made her feel physically sick.

Trying to slow her galloping pulse, she closed her eyes, leaned her head back against the seat and breathed deeply. *No one would stop her.* No one was expecting her.

It had been six months: six months during which she'd learned to live her life looking over her shoulder. No names. No identities. Everything paid in cash. She'd lived a completely anonymous life in order to protect herself.

But now she was back.

In Sicily.

For many, the Mediterranean island was a paradise.

For Chessie it was a prison.

Soon, she thought to herself, shifting restlessly in her seat. Soon she'd do what had to be done. But for now she just wanted to see her mother. It had been six months…

The co-pilot walked into the back of the plane. 'We'll be landing in five minutes, Miss Berkeley. Keep your seat belt fastened. The car is waiting for you, as you requested.' He spoke in heavily accented English, and Chessie replied in the same language, careful to conceal the fact that she was fluent in Italian. For a brief moment she contemplated what the pilot would say if he knew her identity, but then she gave a mental shrug, reassuring herself that there was no way the pilot could identify her. There was nothing in any of her documents that would betray her.

'*Va bene.*' The co-pilot nodded to her. 'Have a safe journey.'

A safe journey?

Discovering that her mouth was dry with fear, Chessie tensed as the plane landed in a series of gentle bumps, and then fumbled with her seat belt, lifted her overnight bag and forced herself to walk to the front of the plane.

It would be all right, she told herself firmly as she walked down the steps onto the tarmac, breathing in the scent of

Sicily and feeling the warmth of the night air close around her. Her father was dead. The funeral had passed. No one was going to be expecting her home. She'd sneak in and see her mother, and then leave.

And then she was going to sort out her life.

No more running.

No more hiding. If nothing else, the last six months had taught her that she was capable of so much more than she'd ever imagined.

In her state of high anxiety, the powerful headlights of the approaching car reminded her of searchlights. Trying to control her galloping imagination and her racing pulse, Chessie tensed as the vehicle purred across the tarmac and gently came to a halt beside her.

Anxious to avoid the attention of anyone who might be watching, she barely waited for the rear door to swing open before she slipped inside.

Only as the door closed behind her, sealing her in, did she realise that there was someone else in the back of the car, and her stomach lurched in a wild panic.

Oh, no, no, *no!*

Frozen by shock, she was unable to move. Unable to look. She didn't *need* to look. She *knew* who it was because she felt his presence with every bone in her body.

Rocco Castellani.

Billionaire and bastard.

Her husband.

Keeping an iron grip on his simmering temper, Rocco watched as she reached for the door handle—watched as she registered the fact that the rear of the car was locked, providing her with no means to escape. Beneath the brim of the hat he could see that her eyes held the panicky, frightened look of a hunted animal.

He'd underestimated her, he thought grimly, and felt a flicker of cynical amusement. Because, of all the women he'd ever met, Francesca was the only one who had ever managed to surprise him.

'*Buona sera, tesoro.* Welcome home.' He switched to English because that was the language they'd always spoken together, and saw the colour drain from her cheeks.

It was obvious that she hadn't expected him to be here, and her reaction intrigued him.

Was she really that naïve?

Had she really thought she could return to Sicily without his knowledge?

He waited for her to say something, but she didn't speak. Instead she sat in frozen stillness, clutching the edge of the seat, her chest rising and falling rapidly as she sucked in air.

If she'd been anyone else Rocco would almost have felt sorry for her.

But he was a long way from feeling sorry for his wife. Why should he? After what she'd done she was fortunate that he was even prepared to sit in the same car as her.

'You look surprised to see me.' With a huge effort he kept his tone neutral, careful to reveal nothing of his true feelings. 'Why? We're married, *tesoro.* Why wouldn't I be here to meet my wife on her return to our home?'

Finally she turned to look at him, and her eyes were stricken. '*How* did you know?' Her voice was little more than a choked whisper, and he had to strain his ears to catch her words.

'How did I know you'd be landing tonight?' The smile didn't come easily but somehow he managed it, along with a casual lift of his shoulders. 'Did you really think I wouldn't?

You're my wife, Francesca. I care about everything that happens to you. Your father entrusted you to me and I'm responsible for your safety. It's a role I take extremely seriously.'

'Care?' Her voice recovered some of its strength. 'You don't care about me, Rocco. You don't care about anyone but yourself.'

Rocco leaned forward and removed the hat. Her dark hair slid from the inadequate clip and tumbled over her shoulders in curling waves. She looked incredibly young. Far too young to be so scheming.

'What a surprise you are,' he murmured thoughtfully. 'So much fire and spirit, and yet you keep it so well hidden. When we met before our wedding you barely spoke. I had to coax every word out of you. I thought you were impossibly shy.'

For a moment she just stared at him. 'You don't know me at all, Rocco.'

'Clearly.' He wondered if she even registered the irony in his tone. 'But I intend to work very hard to rectify that. In fact you should probably know that I now intend to devote all of my time to furthering our acquaintance.'

'No.' There was a note of panic in her voice, and she gave a quick shake of her head. 'You don't need to know me. And I don't want to know you either. I already know enough.'

She was a mass of contradictions, he thought to himself as he studied her. Infinitely complex. First impressions had suggested that she was gentle and timid and yet she'd proved herself to be wild and wilful. 'Your dark hair shows your Italian blood.' He leaned forward and gently wound a silken lock around his finger. 'But those blue eyes of yours show your English heritage.' She had huge sapphire eyes, and a soft pink mouth that was temptingly full. In fact, she was a vision of feminine youth and innocence. And yet he knew that her innocence was gone for ever. Lost to another man. Anger rushed through him, along with another infinitely more ugly and dangerous emotion.

Jealousy.

So this was how it felt, he mused, trying to detach himself from the hot burn of envy that licked at the heels of his iron self control.

This was how it felt to confront infidelity.

Something from his past—*something dark and dangerous*—flickered to life and he ruthlessly suppressed it, reminding himself of his golden rule.

Move forward. Always forward. Never back.

She might have lost her innocence but she was still his.

Her breathing was rapid. 'Don't touch me. I don't want you to touch me.' With a jerk of her head she moved away from his fingers and slid to the furthest corner of the seat, staring straight ahead, as if by not looking at him she could somehow deny his presence. 'I want to go to my father's house.'

Still struggling against a desire to flatten her to the seat and make himself the entire focus of her attentions, Rocco was silent for a moment, his eyes on her profile as he considered her request. 'Aren't you a little late? Your father is dead. The funeral was two weeks ago.' He softened neither his tone nor the harshness of his words, and yet there was no reaction from her. Nothing. It didn't fit, he mused as he watched her. The pieces just didn't slot together. 'As his only child, you didn't think it might be appropriate to show up and pay your respects before now?'

She turned to face him, and there was something in her eyes that he couldn't interpret. 'No,' she said quietly. 'I didn't.'

'Why not?'

There was a long silence—a long silence during which she simply stared at him with a blank expression in her eyes. Then she turned her head away. 'My relationship with my father is none of your business, Rocco. I don't owe you anything, least of all explanations. And I'm not here to see you. I came to see my mother.'

'Your mother has gone.'

'Gone?' There was shock in her voice and fear in her eyes. 'Gone where?'

'I really have no idea,' Rocco drawled, and she reached across the seat and clutched his arm with nervous fingers.

'Was she at the funeral? *I need to know if she was at the funeral.*'

'Yes. She left soon afterwards.' He watched as she sank against the seat, her eyes closed, her relief visible.

'Thank goodness,' she whispered. 'In that case you can stop the car. I'll get back on the plane and I won't bother you again. You can get on with your life.'

'I intend to. But I certainly won't be taking you back to the plane,' Rocco said smoothly. 'We have much to talk about. Welcome home, *tesoro.*'

She was still his, he reminded himself with grim determination.

Everything else was in the past, and he was a master at keeping his eyes fixed firmly on the future.

Much to talk about?

Watching her hope for a rapid departure from Sicily crash and burn, Chessie tried to think fast. *Why hadn't she anticipated this?* How could she have been so stupid as to imagine that she could arrive in Sicily and not be noticed?

At what point had she forgotten just exactly who her husband was?

They called him *il lupo*. The wolf.

He'd made his first million before he was even out of his teens, and then carried on amassing money with ruthless determination. As unpredictable as he was brilliant, he was also wild, ruthless and dangerously handsome. Chessie had once overheard a woman observe in dreamy tones that if the world were about to end, then she'd choose to spend her last night naked with Rocco Castellani.

He was the object of every woman's fantasies, and being this close to him froze her normally agile brain.

Watchful and unsmiling, he lounged back against the seat, his powerful body almost unnaturally still and Chessie found his iron self-control strangely intimidating. Everything about him was dark. His eyes, his hair and his simmering temper. She gave a tiny shiver, because he embodied power and authority, and she knew that this man wielded more influence than her father ever had.

He was the ultimate smooth operator, but she wasn't fooled by the sophisticated persona that Rocco presented to the world. The shockingly expensive hand-made Italian shoes, the exquisitely cut suit and the impossibly handsome face were nothing more than camouflage. A disguise designed to lull his opponents into a false sense of security. She knew that the charismatic smile that had seduced so many willing women hid a cold, tough streak that would have been the envy of the average barracuda.

It didn't matter how this man dressed, or how he appeared to others. She knew the truth.

Rocco Castellani was Sicilian. Full-blooded Sicilian. And Chessie was one of the few people who understood exactly what that meant.

You could wrap a tiger in a sheep's fleece but it would still be a tiger underneath.

His presence in the car was so unexpected that her cool determination deserted her. Her heart took off at an alarming pace and her insides suddenly churned.

'You can't seriously wish to continue with our marriage?' She must have misunderstood him.

The silence stretched between them and she stared at him in panicked silence, finding it impossible to read his expression and equally impossible to look away from his glittering dark eyes.

'Why?'

'Because our marriage is over.' *Because she'd left him.* What Sicilian would forgive that?

He gave a faint smile. 'It hasn't even begun, *tesoro.* Thanks to you, we have much ground to cover. I'm looking forward to it.'

Her heart was pounding like a hammer against her chest, and her whole body was gripped by a reaction so violent she thought she might pass out. 'What are you doing here? *Why a*re you here? The papers said you were in New York.' *She'd been banking on it.*

'You should never believe everything you read in the papers, but I'm flattered to know that you've shown such an interest in my movements during your long holiday.' His voice smooth, his eyes still on her face, he issued a set of instructions to the driver before relaxing back in the seat. 'Clearly you were missing me. Don't be embarrassed. It's perfectly natural for a wife to miss her husband. I'm just relieved that we've now been reunited.' His tone was smooth and civilised, but Chessie felt her palms grow damp—because she wasn't fooled by his outward appearance of calm. Rocco was a deadly opponent, and she knew that her actions had put her in the role of adversary.

He had to be angry. She *knew* he had to be angry. And yet so far he hadn't even raised his voice

'H-how did you know I was on that plane?' Her stammer was back, and she wanted to scream with frustration. Why now? Why, when she needed every bit of her new-found confidence, did everything she'd learned over the past six months suddenly desert her?

'Why wouldn't I know?' His firm, sensual mouth flickered into a faint smile. 'After your father's death, your return to Sicily was inevitable. It was only a matter of time. Patience isn't my major virtue, but I struggled through.'

'I thought I— You didn't—'

'Since you didn't come home for the funeral, I assume you have finally returned because you are bored with your lover.'

'My lover?' She stared at him blankly, still trying to come to terms with the fact that he'd obviously been waiting for her return. 'What lover?' Still in shock, she couldn't look away from his penetrating gaze, and her voice was barely a whisper.

'You're my wife. From the moment we exchanged vows, my security team was briefed to watch you closely. So if you're trying to deny that you left our wedding with Carlo Mancini—' he gave a careless shrug, as if the matter was of little consequence '—then you're wasting your time. I hope you found him a satisfying sexual partner.' Something in the way he delivered those words increased her tension, and she remembered that one of Rocco's most deadly skills was his ability to think with a cool, clear head even when he was seething with anger.

And he *was* seething with anger. She sensed it. *Sensed his inner struggle.*

Unlike her father, Rocco had learned to control his unpredictable Sicilian temperament and use it to his advantage. Instead of confronting the enemy, he studied them, watching for weakness, picking his time to pounce and kill. She'd once read a profile of him in the financial pages of a quality newspaper that had described him as a master of strategy, a skilful tactician and a merciless adversary. He was a man who took no prisoners.

Except her. She had been earmarked to be his prisoner by virtue of their marriage.

It was one of the reasons she'd escaped. One of the reasons she'd taken off with Carlo. Carlo, her father's gardener, who had just happened to be in the right place at the right time. It hadn't occurred to her that Rocco would think they were lovers. In fact that assumption on his part was just another example of the differences between them.

She would no more take a lover on her wedding day than she would swim naked through a pool full of sharks, and the fact that he thought that she would said more about him than it did about her.

He was a man who didn't know the meaning of the word love.

A man who had never cared for a woman in his life.

And she still couldn't believe that she was trapped in the back of his car. She'd been so careful…

'How did you know I was on the plane?' She blurted the words out before she could stop herself. 'I paid them in cash.'

'And I paid them more.' A bored expression on his face, he glanced at his watch. 'Your naïvety is incredibly touching. Did you really think I'd allow my wife to return to Sicily without the appropriate protection? I'm just pleased that you came home alone and didn't bring your boyfriend. That would have been embarrassing for all concerned.'

She curled her hands over the seat, her knuckles whitening, worry suddenly choking all her fragile confidence. He *seriously* thought that Carlo was her lover? Wasn't that just typical of the way the Sicilian male mind worked? Jealousy and possessiveness blinded reason every time, and she understood that his anger stemmed not from love but from the public dent to his pride.

He thought she'd lost her virginity to another man.

For a moment she sat there mute, so unaccustomed to standing up for herself that she didn't know where to begin. And then she remembered exactly what sort of man he was and felt courage flicker to life inside her. If she was going to fight then it had to be now.

Like a diver braced to enter deep water, she drew in a breath and plunged. 'I'm not coming back to you, Rocco. I don't want to be married to you. I want a divorce.' She'd rehearsed the words so many times that they flew from her lips with remarkable ease, and immediately she felt relief.

It was done.

No more lying awake at night, planning the best way to approach him. No more plucking up courage.

'How can you not wish to be married to me,' he drawled softly, 'when the very last time we met you were standing in front of a priest and saying yes to that very question?'

'That was when I thought you were a nice person.'

Amusement flickered in his dark gaze. 'Francesca, *tesoro*, I am a nice person,' he purred softly, thick dark lashes lowering slightly to conceal his expression. 'How could you think otherwise? I'm always kind to old ladies and children.'

'Y-ou don't know any old ladies or children.'

'But if I did—' he gave a dismissive shrug and waved a bronze hand expressively '—I would be kind to them.'

'And then you'd probably rob them,' Chessie choked, turning away from the burning dark gaze that churned her insides into a turmoil. 'You don't think about anyone but yourself.'

'On the contrary, I've thought of little but you since you walked away from our wedding. Do I need to remind you that you couldn't wait to marry me? You had stars in your eyes from the moment I proposed. You were madly in love with me.'

A hot flush of humiliation engulfed her body, and she opened her mouth to utter a denial but it wouldn't come. How could she give voice to such a blatant lie? She *had* been in love with him. It was just that love hadn't been part of her plan. To begin with, marriage to Rocco had just seemed like the perfect escape from her father. It had been a chance to finally gain the freedom she'd craved for so long.

And then they'd spent time together and she'd done what every other woman did when they met Rocco—fallen for his dark, dangerous charm. It was something that she'd never told him, and the fact that he'd *known* how she'd felt about him made her want to slide underneath the nearest rock with embarrassment.

How he must have laughed at her, she thought to herself, looking out of the window to hide her misery. Rocco was a man who had models and actresses competing for his attention. Why would a clumsy, awkward girl who'd never been allowed to travel out of her local village have had a chance of snagging his attention?

'I thought I was in love with you, yes, that's true. But that was before I understood the sort of man you are. I could never love someone like you.'

She blurted out the words, anguish almost choking her. She didn't want to betray just how much she cared, but she couldn't help it. She'd held her feelings inside for so long that her body and brain felt as though they might burst. 'You did what it took to make me say yes, but for you it was all a business arrangement, and that isn't the sort of marriage I want. I want the real thing!'

'The real thing?' The mockery in his voice revealed what

he thought of her statement. 'You're wearing my ring on your finger. How much more real does it get?'

'You just don't understand, do you?' She turned her head and forced herself to look at her husband. *The husband she'd run from.* 'It isn't about rings and vows, Rocco. That's all meaningless. It's about *feelings.* It's about caring and love— all the things you know *nothing* about.'

'And is that what Carlo offered you? Caring and love?' The sarcasm in his tone was the final straw.

'You are a total hypocrite! *Why* did I leave our wedding, Rocco? Have you even bothered asking yourself that question?' She saw his eyes narrow slightly but was unable to stop herself. The anger rose inside her, strengthening her shaking limbs and her flagging confidence. 'How *dare* you sit there and accuse me of having a lover, *mocking me,* when you had the gall to invite your g-girlfriend to our wedding? What sort of man does that, Rocco? What sort of man expects his girlfriend to watch him marrying another woman? What sort of man expects his new wife to entertain his mistress? Don't you have any feelings? Don't you have any morals—?'

She broke off, shocked by her own outburst and suddenly apprehensive. Living with her father, she'd spent her entire life biting her tongue, keeping her eyes on the floor and never answering back. Never before this moment had she spoken her mind. Instinctively she shrank back in her seat, but he made no move towards her, only continued to watch her, one dark eyebrow raised in sardonic appraisal.

'That is the longest speech I've ever heard you make,' he observed in a lazy drawl. 'When we spent time together before the wedding you were virtually monosyllabic. Impossibly shy. I had to work overtime to get any sort of response from you. You stared at the floor, the walls, the table—anywhere but at me. It's fascinating to note that you do, in fact, have an opinion.'

She blushed fiercely, knowing that what he said was true. Almost all their meetings had been carried out in the presence of her father, and she'd learned from bitter experience that it was safer to stay silent than risk incurring his anger. She'd learned how not to draw attention to herself.

'Well, I'm looking at you now and I'm speaking now,' she said, trying to keep her voice steady. There was no way she was going to show him how nervous she felt. 'And my opinion of you is rock bottom, Rocco. You measure everything in terms of profit. You don't do anything unless you gain something from it. And you don't care about people's feelings. I've had six months to think about what you did. You married me because you wanted my father's business. That was bad enough, but I thought that you at least had some respect for me. And then *you invited your mistress to our wedding*!'

The pain and humiliation still throbbed inside her like a raw and vicious wound.

'You're being extremely juvenile. There were two hundred guests at our wedding.'

'I don't care about the two hundred. Just about the one. The tall blonde one who couldn't put you down. Your girlfriend!'

'Ex-girlfriend,' he corrected her, with a faint frown. 'And I don't know what you're worrying about. She and I weren't together any more.'

'So why were you kissing her on the terrace?'

He suppressed a yawn, visibly bored by the conversation. 'I can't honestly remember. Some women are naturally affectionate. She was probably kissing me goodbye.'

Naturally affectionate? Chessie recalled the driven passion of that kiss—recalled the envy that had almost floored her.

Rocco had never kissed her like that. 'If you weren't together then why did you even invite her?'

His eyes grew suddenly cold. 'Your position as my wife doesn't give you the right to question my behaviour. Frankly, I don't understand what you have to complain about. I married you. You were the lucky one.'

It took a few moments for his arrogant statement to penetrate her brain. 'Lucky? Lucky?' She stared at him in disbelief, searching his bronzed, handsome face for some evidence of remorse or contrition. But there was nothing except confidence and authority. This was not a man given to questioning his own actions.

'Yes, lucky,' he drawled softly. 'I offered you something that I have never offered another woman.'

'And that was supposed to make me feel how, exactly?'

'Grateful?'

'Grateful?' She choked on the word. 'Grateful to be given the opportunity to share my husband with half a dozen others? Well, excuse me if I'm not displaying the correct level of gratitude!'

'I never would have guessed you had a fraction of this much passion locked up inside you. How intriguing. It does explain a great deal.' His gaze was thoughtful as he studied her face. 'But you probably ought to know that jealousy is not a trait that I find appealing in a woman. And your jealousy is ridiculous, given that *you* are the one wearing my ring.'

'I'm not jealous. To be jealous I would have to care, and I really don't care about you one little bit.' *Once she had. Once she'd been ecstatic at the thought of marrying him.* So excited that she hadn't been able to wipe the smile from her face. But that had all been a childish fantasy. The reality had proved to be entirely different. 'I wasn't jealous. I was humiliated.

Publicly. What was I supposed to do, Rocco? Was I supposed to look at all those women drooling over you and feel blessed? Is that what you're saying? I was expected to party with your cast-offs and smile because I was the chosen one? Is that right?'

He watched her through half-shut eyes. 'You're hysterical.'

'No, Rocco. I'm *not* hysterical. I'm thinking clearly for the first time in years.' And she no longer cared about the consequences of speaking out. Where had silence ever got her? 'Answer me one question. If you wanted to be with that blonde girl then why didn't you just marry her and have done with it?'

'Lorna is American. She wouldn't have made a suitable wife. She has her own business and she's very independent.'

'What sort of an answer is that?' Chessie gaped at him in disbelief. 'What you mean is that she had more sense than to marry you! So instead you thought you'd choose some dumb Sicilian girl who didn't know any better? Is that what you're trying to say? Well, someone should have reminded you that my mother was English, so my Sicilian blood is rather diluted. You made a mistake marrying me, Rocco. A big one.'

His hard gaze didn't flicker. 'I never make mistakes. You, on the other hand, made an enormous one by leaving our marriage. But you're back now, so you can start making amends. I've decided to overlook the fact that you're no longer a virgin. Play your cards right and I might even forgive you.'

Forgive *her*? She stared at him in helpless frustration. He didn't even believe he'd done anything wrong. Rocco Castellani was so used to treating women badly that he didn't even realise there was any other way. He was *just* like her father. A wife was someone to leave at home while he went out partying with other women.

'I'm sure you found plenty of willing females to console you.' Chessie was mortified to discover that she had a lump in her throat. Why did she care? Why did she care that their wedding had meant so little to him? It was over. Their marriage was over, and she felt nothing for him except contempt.

His eyes were cold. 'You agreed to the wedding. It was what you wanted.'

'That was before I knew the truth about you.'

'What truth is that?'

Her breath caught and for a moment she hesitated, almost too embarrassed to admit her own naïvety. But there were times for honesty, she reminded herself, and this was one of them. 'You and my father set me up. You both treated me like some sort of commodity.' She stumbled over the word and lifted a hand to her throat to try and slow her breathing. 'You bartered and bargained until you both got what you wanted. You made me think that you wanted to marry me, but I was nothing more than a bargaining chip. Not once did either of you stop to think about me. You didn't think about what *I* wanted. What *I* needed. It was all about *you*.'

And she'd been torn apart by their lack of care and their naked ambition.

'Plenty of marriages are arranged in such a way, and we were not strangers. You seem to be conveniently forgetting the time we spent together. We spent many hours getting to know one another.' He spoke the words with subtle emphasis, and she knew exactly what he was referring to.

That one occasion when curiosity had defeated modesty and common sense and she'd kissed him.

It had been an experience that had disturbed her sleep ever since. *The warm, sensual pressure of his mouth against hers. The slow, lazy stroke of his strong hand over her trembling thigh.* The sudden eruption of sensations in her body had been so shockingly exciting that she'd hoped that he'd strip her naked there and then and satisfy her female curiosity in full.

But he hadn't.

And now she knew why. He hadn't found her attractive. He'd married her for other reasons entirely.

But she hadn't been able to forget that one kiss, and even now her body flared hot at the memory and she felt her nipples harden. Without thinking, she let her eyes drop to his mouth, and she felt something warm and dangerous uncurl low in her pelvis.

Horrified by the almost painful intensity of her reaction, she lifted her eyes to his, saw the gleam of masculine understanding in his sardonic gaze and looked away quickly.

'I didn't get to know you at all.' Embarrassed by the reaction of her body, she was grateful for the black coat that covered her. 'You revealed nothing of yourself, Rocco. As far as you were concerned, those meetings of ours were no more than a job interview.'

'Job interview?' There was a trace of humour in his tone as he repeated her words. 'And what was the job?'

'Your wife. Salary: unlimited. Bonus and perks: amazing. Requirements: one meek, obedient virgin who will stay at home, do as she is told and never answer back.' She couldn't stop her gaze sliding to his mouth. *The same mouth that had kissed her just the once.* Then she remembered that it was also the same mouth that had been kissing his mistress on their wedding day. 'A girl who is prepared to be understanding and tolerant about your numerous affairs. Well, you chose the wrong woman for the job. I resign. Next time you marry, you might want to extend the interview process, Rocco.'

'Why would I want to marry again when I have a perfectly good wife sitting in front of me?' His silky observation caused a flicker of shock to whip through her body and she stared at him, careful to hide her consternation.

He was joking. He had to be joking. No way would a proud, arrogant man like Rocco allow his wife to leave on their wedding day and then take her back.

He was going to release her. She knew he would.

He would make it difficult and awkward, but eventually he would release her.

She'd finally be free.

'You're just saying that to punish me because your ego is damaged.'

His smile indicated just how much that statement amused him. 'My ego is completely intact. Why wouldn't it be?'

'You can't possibly want to stay married to me. We both know that you only married me in the first place because it was part of the deal you agreed with my father.' It felt so humiliating to admit the truth—*to admit that he hadn't found her in the slightest bit attractive.* Obviously that had been the reason that he'd held back when they'd kissed. He'd been postponing the moment when he'd have to make love to her. 'My father needed someone to run his company and you were the chosen one. And why were you chosen? Because you were the only man he'd ever met who was as ruthless as he was himself. Congratulations.'

Rocco raised an eyebrow. 'By *ruthless* I assume you mean possessing the ability to make a decision unaffected by emotions—a concept that most women find impossible to grasp.'

'Emotions are important, Rocco. You and my father each had your own agenda to follow. The only one that neither of you bothered to think about was *me*. All you thought about was your own greed.' And she couldn't believe she'd been stupid enough to fall in love with him.

'Your father's company was losing money, so I can hardly be accused of greed.' He gave a casual shrug. 'Generosity, possibly.'

Shocked into silence by that unexpected statement, Chessie stared at him. 'It was losing money?'

'Why does that surprise you? Your father's olive oil business was very much a local operation, and he had no idea how to expand or make himself competitive.'

'My father's business was successful.' She thought of all the important people who had come to the villa; *of the deference they'd shown towards her father.*

'Your father's business was corrupt and badly run,' Rocco interjected, his tone suddenly hard. 'His methods were locked in the Dark Ages. But I'm slowly rectifying that.'

Chessie shook her head, trying to take in the enormity of what he was saying. 'Are you seriously telling me that my father's business was failing?'

'You didn't know?'

'Why would I know? My father never discussed business with me,' Chessie said stiffly. 'I picked the olives and I did some of his secretarial work but he never shared the details with me. Had I been a boy it would have been different, but as it was—'

'—he had a daughter.' Rocco's gaze rested on her face thoughtfully, as if something had just occurred to him.

'I don't understand.' She stared at him blankly. 'If my father's company was such a disaster, why would you want it?'

'Call it a whim.' Rocco gave a faint smile that revealed nothing. 'A sentimental desire to have a touch of Sicily in my portfolio of companies.'

'You're about as sentimental as a man-eating lion.'

His smile widened. 'You think so? All right, in that case I

admit it may have had more to do with profit than sentiment. I have a talent for spotting commercial opportunities that others have missed.' His eyes were suddenly sharp, his tone crisp. 'Your father was losing business because of the weaknesses in his operation, not because of the produce. The oil is top quality. I've eaten in the best restaurants all over the world and I've never tasted better. I'm going to export the oil as a premium product.'

Chessie stared at him. She'd grown up with olives, and she was completely unable to get excited about them. Harvesting them from the bushes was hard work. 'The market is flooded with olive oil.'

Rocco gaze lingered on her mouth. 'Not *my* olive oil,' he said with gentle emphasis. 'There's always a market for the best, and extra virgin oil is the best.'

Wishing that he'd stop looking at her in that lazy, assessing way, Chessie felt her colour rise. 'That's a typically Sicilian male remark,' she muttered. 'Even the oil has to be virgin. And not just virgin, but *extra* virgin.'

He moved so quickly that she didn't see it coming. One minute he was lounging at a safe distance, the next his dangerously handsome face was close to hers. 'If I were obsessed with virgins,' he purred softly, 'then I wouldn't have gone to the trouble of drawing you back into the folds of matrimony once you'd lost yours.' He lifted a hand and slid his fingers over her cheek, forcing her to look at him. 'And if I were typically Sicilian I would have put an end to that spotty teenager you ran off with on our wedding day. I'm trying to be *incredibly civilised* about the whole thing, but, just for the record, it probably isn't a good idea to remind me that you were unfaithful. From now on it's a banned topic of conversation.'

Chessie stared at him, unable to move, hypnotised by the darkness of his eyes and the thickness of his lashes.

He was so good-looking it almost hurt to look at him.

Her heart pounded, and she struggled against an almost irresistible urge to press her mouth to his. 'Why did you marry me? It sounds as though my father should have paid *you* to take the business off his hands.'

For a moment he stared down at her in brooding silence, and she wondered whether he was feeling the same inexplicable urge as she was. Then he slid back along the seat, putting distance between them. 'I was ready for marriage. If I hadn't been then I would never have agreed to your father's demands, no matter how much I wanted access to his olive oil.'

He'd been ready for marriage? Chessie gaped at him, and thought of everything she'd ever read about him. His reputation with women was scorching hot. Rocco Castellani certainly wasn't known for monogamy. If he'd been ready for marriage, then he'd certainly hidden it well. 'So why didn't you marry one of your many willing mistresses?'

'What a quaint expression. Very Victorian England.' He gave a faint smile as he acknowledged the term. 'A mistress is for sex, *tesoro*. Metaphorically speaking, all a mistress is required to do is set fire to the bed. The position of wife, however, carries entirely different responsibilities, and for that I wanted a different type of woman. I wanted a Sicilian girl.'

'I'm half-English.'

'Your father was Sicilian and you were brought up in Sicily.' He gave a casual shrug. 'That's good enough for me.'

'You mean because I'm supposed to know what's expected of a Sicilian wife?' She straightened her back and lifted her chin, remembering all the times she'd rehearsed this scenario. 'Well, I've got news for you. I would make a really, *really* bad

Sicilian wife. You better divorce me quickly, Rocco, before I display too much of my English blood.'

His powerful frame stilled. 'One final time—I have no intention of divorcing you. Ever. I don't believe in divorce. You are my wife and you're staying as my wife. The sooner you get used to the idea, the more comfortable for both of us.'

CHAPTER TWO

HE HAD no intention of divorcing her?

Chessie sat in frozen silence, wondering if she'd misunderstood him. *Hoping.* She'd always known that one day she'd come face to face with Rocco again, but she'd consoled herself with the knowledge that, however bad the confrontation, ultimately he'd agree to a divorce. His behaviour at their wedding had proved that he had absolutely no thought or care for her. That their wedding meant nothing to him in emotional terms.

He had the business now. Her father was dead.

Why would he possibly want to stay married to her?

'We can have a quick, quiet divorce,' she said quickly. 'I don't want any money or anything, and I won't make a fuss.'

'You can forget it,' he drawled, his eyes hard. 'There's no way I'm giving you a divorce. So if your lover is waiting in the wings to marry you then I hope he's a patient man.'

She opened her mouth to deny that Carlo was her lover, and then closed it again, her brain sprinting into overdrive.

Rocco was pure-bred Sicilian, driven by macho tendencies and a possessive nature designed to control and dominate.

Surely the one thing that would eventually push him

towards divorce was confirmation that she'd been with another man?

It was a high-risk strategy, but…

'Carlo and I don't care about marriage,' she said quietly, carefully watching his reaction. 'We just want to be together.'

Something hard and dangerous glinted in his black eyes, but when he spoke his voice was steady. 'Then you can resign yourself to misery, because as far as I'm concerned marriage is for life.'

'Why, when you say it, does that prospect sound so completely unromantic?' She gave a humourless laugh and shook her head slightly. 'I get a prison sentence while you go off and enjoy yourself. My father married my mother for "life", so I understand exactly what that means to a Sicilian man. Forget it, Rocco. Once, maybe, there was a chance for us. But you blew it when you invited that girl to our wedding. If you couldn't even manage to stay faithful on your wedding day, then what chance is there for us?'

'I don't think you're in a position to lecture me about morals,' he observed in a silky tone, and she closed her eyes briefly, aware that she'd fallen into a trap of her own making.

All she could do now was play on his possessive streak.

'I'm not a virgin. I've had sex, Rocco. Lots of it. Do you really want a woman who is thinking of another man?'

His powerful body stilled, and for a brief moment she wondered if she'd gone too far. 'That's in the past. It will take less than fifteen seconds in my bed for you to forget you ever knew anyone else,' he predicted with characteristic arrogance. 'By the time I've finished with you the only name you'll be crying out is mine.'

She blushed hotly, unutterably shocked by the vivid image created in her mind. 'I can't believe you just said that.'

'Try and be consistent, *cara mia*,' he advised in a silky tone. 'You can't flaunt your lover one minute and then pretend modesty the next. Make up your mind. Which are you? Virgin or vamp?'

Virgin, she wanted to shriek, but she knew that wouldn't help her case. 'You can't make me stay here,' she said in a strangled voice. 'I only came back to see my mother. If she isn't here then I'm leaving.'

'You're not leaving. You're my wife. And as soon as we reach my villa I'm going to remind you of that fact.'

Was he seriously going to overlook her claim that she wasn't a virgin?

No, that wasn't possible.

Her heart performed a series of elaborate acrobatics and suddenly she realised that she didn't have a clue what to do next. She wasn't used to playing games, least of all with men like Rocco. He was totally out of her league.

Suddenly she regretted the impulse that had driven her to lie. 'You're just trying to stake your claim, like some sort of male predator marking his territory. But you don't need to. I was lying when I said I had an affair with Carlo. The truth is that I hardly knew Carlo. I—I just said that because I thought it would make you divorce me.'

'Nothing will make me divorce you, and changing your story every three seconds isn't going to change that fact.' Rocco's eyes didn't shift from her face. 'I've already said that I don't want his name mentioned, but this once—just this once—we'll examine the facts together so that there can be no mistake. You ran away with him on our wedding day. You now expect me to believe that the relationship was innocent?'

'He gave me a lift, that's all. He was saving me!'

'Saving you?' One dark eyebrow rose in sardonic appraisal. 'From what, precisely, *tesoro*? A life of rich, pampered idleness? More money than you could ever dream of spending? A fleet of staff waiting to supply your every need?'

She gazed at him with frustration and disbelief. He was *exactly* like her father. He measured everything in terms of wealth and possessions. If it couldn't be bought, it wasn't worth having.

'I don't care about any of those things.' For a moment she was tempted to blurt out the truth. She was tempted to tell him that what she wanted most in life was freedom. But she knew that a man like Rocco Castellani would never understand. What could he possibly know about her life? What could he know about growing up as her father's daughter? 'I decided that I just couldn't be married to you.' *To a man who was so careless of her feelings.*

'You preferred to run off with a spotty teenager,' he observed, in a slow, masculine drawl that dragged at her nerve-endings. 'Did he satisfy you, *tesoro*? Was your first experience of sex the stuff of dreams? I remember that first time in your father's garden, when I kissed you. Or did you kiss me? I can't remember the exact circumstances. All I remember is your warm body pressing against mine, urging me on.'

He'd known.

The colour flooded into her cheeks and she felt a sudden heat in her body. He'd known *exactly* what that one, single kiss had done to her—how desperate and frustrated she'd felt. The knowledge that he'd understood her so well simply increased her feelings of humiliation. She'd made *such* a fool of herself. Once she'd believed that he found her attractive. She'd believed that he cared about her as a person. But then she'd discovered that he wouldn't have cared *who* she was.

The only thing he'd cared about was sealing the deal with her father and gaining a traditional, Sicilian wife.

It was her parents' relationship all over again.

Why hadn't she seen it sooner?'

Before the wedding she'd been dizzy with happiness. For the first time in years she'd seen a glimmer of light in what had been a bleak, dark future. She was finally escaping from her father. And she was marrying the man of a million women's dreams. Rocco was an international businessman. She'd finally get to leave Sicily. She'd travel. She'd have a life outside the villa.

Her battered confidence and her trampled self-esteem had made a brief recovery as she'd imagined her new life. No more being insignificant and lonely. As Rocco's wife she'd be welcomed everywhere. She was going to glitter and shine. All those skinny girls at the convent school she'd attended, who had mocked and teased her about her height and her curves, would stare in awe and envy as she married the most eligible bachelor in the western world.

Rocco Castellani had chosen *her*.

He'd looked beyond her tallness and her womanly figure and her hideously shy exterior and seen the woman she really was.

Or so she'd believed.

Remembering just how completely she'd deluded herself, she wanted to shrink with humiliation. How could she have been so pitifully desperate?

'Let's not play games. It's demeaning to both of us.' She could hardly bring herself to say the words. It was just so deeply embarrassing. 'You didn't want to marry me. Tell me honestly, Rocco, just how much did my father pay you to take me off his hands?'

His gaze didn't shift. 'I spend enough of my day talking about business. I don't want to do it with my wife.'

'Business?' Her voice rose and suddenly she forgot her nerves. '*Business?* This was our *wedding*, Rocco. It wasn't supposed to be about business. It was about two people pledging to spend their lives together.'

'I made that pledge.'

He made it sound like just another one of his deals, and she turned her head away so that the pain wouldn't show in her eyes. There was absolutely no way she wanted him to see just how much she was hurting. *Just how much the deal had humiliated her.*

'Fine. Well, my father gave you the company on our wedding day, so you got what you wanted.'

He gave a wry smile. 'So far I've spent twenty-three hours a day trying to unravel the mess that your father called a business. Things are finally showing a positive improvement. I'm now ready to turn my attention to our marriage.'

Chessie stared at him, hypnotised by the look in his dark eyes. Her heart skipped and danced and her thighs felt heavy. Something uncurled deep inside her, and she quickly dragged her gaze away from his, confused by her reaction.

She didn't feel anything, she told herself firmly. She really didn't. It was just that he was incredibly good-looking and it was hard to forget that. *Hard to look at him and not think about sex.*

Dragging her gaze away from his, she stared out of the window, suddenly aware that she'd paid no attention to her surroundings. From the moment she'd stepped into the car and seen him lounging on the seat next to her, her brain had frozen. 'Where are we going, anyway?'

'Home, of course. Where else would a married couple spend their time? We need somewhere that we can be completely alone and undisturbed.' His voice was a soft purr. 'My villa is the most private place I know. And you and I really do need privacy to get to know each other better, *cara mia*.'

There was no mistaking the implication behind his words, and she turned to him, a flush on her cheeks. 'Why? Is your current girlfriend busy?'

'That is an *extremely* childish comment.'

The car drew to a halt and Chessie realised that they were at a marina. 'Where are we?'

'You don't recognise it?' He gave a faint frown, as if surprised by her question, and she wondered what he'd say if he knew she'd never been allowed to travel further than the local village, deep in the Sicilian countryside.

'I've never been here.'

'That surprises me, because your home isn't far from here.' His eyes rested on her thoughtfully, and then he gave a tiny shrug as he named the harbour town. 'My villa is not on the mainland. It's just a short boat trip across the bay. Sufficient to remind you that there is going to be water between you and the rest of the world. Don't even think about returning to your lover.'

'You live on an island?' She hadn't even thought to ask. Her heart plummeted as her last hopes of escape evaporated in front of her hungry eyes. 'I don't want to be trapped on another island!' On an island she'd have no freedom at all. Everything she'd hoped to do, *the person she'd planned to be*—all that would be impossible. 'I've had enough of islands to last me a lifetime. I don't want to be surrounded by water! I want to go to the mainland and have new experiences. I want to—'

'Being in my bed is going to be an experience previously unmatched,' Rocco promised in a low, masculine tone. 'And I can assure you that our surroundings are entirely irrelevant.

All I really need is a locked door, behind which I can remind you that you're my bride. When I've finished with you the only thing you're going to want surrounding you is me.'

She swallowed hard, trying to ignore the burning heat that flared low in her pelvis. 'How can you say that?'

'Why not? It's the truth.'

'You have a ridiculously high opinion of yourself.' Her heart was thudding and her palms were damp. 'You really think you're the ultimate lover, don't you?'

A faint smile touched the corners of his hard mouth. 'I'm naturally competitive, that's true. I always have to be the best at everything I do. What's the point of doing it, otherwise?'

She struggled to keep her voice light. 'Well, much as I hate to dent your ego, Rocco, you ought to know that you do absolutely nothing for me. I prefer my men gentle.'

'I can be extremely gentle.'

A dangerous warmth spread through her limbs, and Chessie struggled to keep her mind on the facts. 'I'm really not turned on by arrogant Sicilians.'

'You're not turned on?' His voice was a deep, accented drawl, and he leaned towards her, his mouth hovering tantalisingly close to hers. His thick dark lashes lowered slightly, and the expression in his eyes was impossible to read. 'You're not at all turned on?'

'Not at all.' She pressed her thighs together ignoring the sudden heat that flared through her body. 'Not even the slightest bit. You do nothing for me.'

His eyes slid to her mouth, lingered there for a torturous moment, and then he smiled and leaned back against his seat. 'I don't know what that fumbling teenage boy of yours taught you, but by the time the sun comes up you're going to be helpless in my bed, *cara mia*. A shivering mass of female gratitude. You're going to plead for me again and again. Play your cards right and I just might indulge you.'

'You arrogant bastard!' Goaded past the point of reason, Chessie lifted a hand and slapped him hard across the face.

'Madre de Dio.' He caught her wrist in his hand, his eyes flashing with a volcanic fury that made her shrink away from him in an instinctive gesture of self-defence.

She couldn't believe the boldness of her actions. In fact, if it hadn't been for the hot sting of her palm and the livid streak of colour on his bronzed cheek, she might have thought that the violence had been all in her imagination.

How many times had she lain there at night, imagining what it would be like to stand up for herself? To be brave and bold? How many times had she imagined herself fighting back? Defending herself and her mother from her father?

In reality she'd only ever done it once, and her defiance had caused repercussions that she'd never forgotten. From that point onwards she had learned to stare at the floor so that the anger in her eyes would never show. And she'd learned to dig her nails into her palms rather than hit out.

Until today.

She braced herself for some degree of retaliation on his part, but, although Rocco's long, strong fingers wrapped around her wrists like bands of iron, he didn't hurt her.

'Let me go.' She tugged hard but he didn't release her. 'And don't expect me to apologise. You deserved that. I'm just amazed no woman has hit you before.'

'Clearly we're going to enjoy an extremely physical relationship, and that's fine by me.'

She yanked at her wrists, her expression frustrated. 'Let go of me! Even you can't force me onto that boat, Rocco! If you try and make me, I'll scream. I'll tell them you're kidnapping me. I'll—' The words died in her throat as his mouth came down on hers with purposeful intent.

The heat of his kiss deprived her of the power of speech and she sank against him, her hands clutching his jacket for support. She felt the intimate invasion of his tongue, the erotic brush of his fingers against her cheek, and the world spun and whirled into a vortex of sensuality from which there was no escape. The feelings released inside her were so incredibly intense that she couldn't think or breathe. Instead she tumbled down and down, falling deeper into a world where the only thing that mattered was satisfaction.

Attempting to relieve the throbbing, insistent ache between her thighs, she slid her arms round his broad shoulders and wriggled closer to him. His mouth still seducing hers, he slid an arm under her legs and lifted her onto his lap in a powerful movement, his arm anchoring her against him. Buttons sprang from her coat as he dragged it open, and then he ripped the thin fabric of her blouse with characteristic impatience.

'You're wearing far too many clothes,' he muttered against her mouth. 'Don't do it again.'

She opened her mouth to tell him not to order her about, but then his clever fingers brushed against her exposed nipple and she cried out as an agonising shaft of excitement pierced her body.

He muttered something in Italian, slid his free hand into her hair to hold her face steady, and claimed her mouth with his once again. This time the kiss went on and on, the excitement heightened by the skilled caress of his fingers. Drained of all resistance, Chessie tumbled further and further into the dark temptation of passion, and when he finally lifted his head she was dazed and shaken—too shaken even to summon a protest when he lifted her into his arms and carried her through the warm night air towards the boat.

Dimly she heard a male voice mutter a coarse observation in Italian, and she heard Rocco's lazy, masculine response.

'Rocco—' Her voice was hoarse, and she squirmed slightly but he held her tightly as he stepped onto the gangplank and issued a series of instructions in rapid Italian. Then he carried her below deck to an elegant living area.

'Sorry to interrupt the fun, but we need to make a move. We'll be on the island in less than twenty minutes. Then we'll be able to take up from where we left off.' Depositing her onto the sofa, he strode across to a cabinet and poured himself a drink. She couldn't help noticing that his hand was totally steady. In fact he looked cool and in control, as if he'd just completed a business meeting.

Unlike her.

She was horrified and confused by her reaction. She didn't like him. She didn't like a single thing about him. And yet when he'd kissed her she'd forgotten everything.

Was she really that shallow?

Infuriated with herself, and hideously self-conscious about the fact that she was now half naked, Chessie wriggled on the sofa and tried to cover herself by closing her coat over her torn blouse. It was only now that she realised he'd somehow managed to remove her bra, and her full breasts were spilling out of the flimsy fabric.

'You've torn my clothes.'

'Buy more. Or, better still, don't wear any. I'm going to be removing them anyway, and my villa is extremely private.'

'You expect me to walk around naked?'

He gave a shrug, casually indifferent. 'Naked works for me when we're the only two people around.'

But it didn't work for her. She hated her body and she always had. At school she'd been the opposite of all her stick-thin friends, and she'd died a thousand deaths from embarrassment. She'd longed to be flat-chested and slim-hipped, but had been blessed with the complete opposite.

Still shivering from the effects of his kiss, she watched in silence as he drank from his glass, trying to ignore the insistent throb of her body. *What had happened to her?* One minute she'd been ready to scream, and the next she'd been unable to string a sentence together. How pathetic was that?

She was furious with herself for reacting in such a predictable way!

'So I'm your prisoner now?' Her voice was hoarse and her fingers clutched the front of her coat together.

'No, *cara mia,*' he said softly, lifting his drink to his lips. 'You're my wife, and I want you to remember that fact and start behaving accordingly.'

Her chin lifted. 'Did *you* remember it at our wedding?'

'My girlfriend isn't here now,' he pointed out. 'So you have me all to yourself. You can look forward to being on the receiving end of my undivided attention.'

She sank back onto the sofa, her heart pounding. She didn't *want* his undivided attention. The thought brought turmoil to her insides. She sought comfort from the knowledge that Rocco was a businessman of international repute, and he hadn't gained that reputation by sequestering himself on a remote Mediterranean island. Sooner or later he'd leave, and so would she. *In the opposite direction.* Even if she had to swim, she wasn't going to stay trapped in Sicily. 'When are you returning to New York?'

He gave a faint smile. 'When I'm bored with sex?'

'If you expect me to believe that you're prepared to

abandon your business in favour of our marriage, then you must think I'm stupid.'

'I didn't say anything about abandoning my business.' There was amusement in his gaze. 'This is the age of technology and hi-tech communication, *tesoro*. I have everything I need to work from the island. For the next few weeks nothing need disturb us, except perhaps the need to eat in between bouts of passionate lovemaking.'

She scrambled to her feet, thoroughly unsettled by the gleam in his eyes and the smile on his lips. 'How can you talk about it so casually? Marriage to you is having a good, obedient wife who is going to stay at home and keep the fire burning.'

Rocco studied her face for a moment and then put his drink down. 'And what is marriage to you?'

'It's a partnership. It's about respect and lo—' She broke off, realising that speaking the word 'love' in front of a man like Rocco would just be to risk exposing herself to ridicule. 'Lots of things like that,' she finished lamely.

'Respect? Is that the same respect you showed me when you left our wedding with another man?' Rocco's voice was deceptively calm. 'For your information, my staff are very excited about welcoming my new bride onto the island. Please remember that.'

In other words, she wasn't to embarrass him.

A thought suddenly occurred to her and she frowned. 'But surely they know we've been separated for the past six months? Everyone knows we haven't been together.'

'No one knows.' He drained the glass. 'I returned to New York the night of our wedding. Everyone, including your father, assumed you were with me.'

'My father thought I was with you?'

'Of course. You gave no thought to anyone but yourself

when you ran off that night.' His voice hardened. 'Your father was in poor health, and yet you left without a word. He died without being given the opportunity to say goodbye to you. Family should be the most important thing in the world, and yet you didn't even attend his funeral.'

Chessie stood still, frozen to the spot. Rocco Castellani had no idea. *He had absolutely no idea what her life had been like.*

She sank back onto the sofa, staring into the distance.

'It is a little late for guilt, *tesoro*.' Rocco's voice penetrated her thoughts. 'Your father is gone. It is too late to make amends.'

'Make amends?' Her voice cracked as she tried to speak. She ought to tell him. She ought to tell him what sort of man her father had really been. But she couldn't even bring herself to speak of it. She was so used to keeping her thoughts completely private that she had absolutely no idea how to confide in anyone, least of all an arrogant Sicilian who was exactly like her father in almost every way. For all she knew, he might approve of her father's conduct.

Suddenly depression and panic mingled inside her.

Marriage to Rocco had freed her from her father, but now she was essentially a prisoner again. Passed from one ruthless man to another.

What was the phrase they used? Out of the frying pan into the fire?

She was only too aware that the flames were well and truly licking around her ankles, waiting to consume her.

'Rocco—'

'The past is behind us. All that matters now is the future.' He reached out a hand and hauled her to her feet. 'We've arrived. Welcome to your new home. The sun is rising and I have some important calls to make. I had to leave New York in rather a hurry. Go to bed and get some rest. You're going to need it.'

CHAPTER THREE

ROCCO toyed with his second glass of wine, watching his new wife across the table that had been laid on the terrace, careful to conceal the anger and frustration that simmered inside him.

They'd arrived at his villa just as the sun rose above the horizon, and he had left his bride sleeping and spent the day trying to unravel the millions of problems that had developed since his departure from New York. He was on the verge of closing another major deal, and his senior executives were in a state of high tension. Whichever way he looked at it, it wasn't a good time to be closeted in Sicily.

Neither was it a good time to risk leaving his bride.

He sensed instinctively that if he left her she'd run again. Or worse. She might contact her lover. Who would have thought she'd be this complicated?

Rocco ground his teeth angrily and topped up his wine glass.

She was a mass of contradictions.

To look at her she seemed innocent and incredibly young. Her dark hair was caught up by a ribbon at the back of her head, and her clothes were extremely demure and wouldn't have looked out of place in the convent school she'd supposedly attended. On the surface she appeared to be the woman he'd chosen to marry. Modest. Warm. A good girl. The perfect wife.

Not someone who would run away with another man on her wedding day.

But since he'd apprehended her at the airport he'd seen an entirely different side to her. Gone was the shy, tongue-tied young woman he'd had to coax into speech. That version of Francesca had been quiet and subservient, pathetically grateful for his attentions. In her place was a fiery, defiant young woman who clearly had a mind of her own. It was as if she'd suddenly discovered that she had an opinion and was determined to express it.

He'd definitely underestimated her, Rocco conceded. Something he never did. But it wouldn't happen again. Already he'd made complex arrangements to guarantee her security. His wife wouldn't be travelling anywhere without his agreement.

He was still smarting over the fact that she'd managed to disappear for six entire months.

Within moments of her stepping into the car with Carlo Mancini, he'd received a full report from his security team. Unfortunately not full enough for him to be able to prevent her departure or track her down.

They'd lost her.

She'd somehow managed to blend into the background and elude his usually eagle-eyed security team.

Rocco gritted his teeth as he reflected on how many staff he'd fired over that incident.

His expression grim, he stared moodily into his wine glass and recalled the occasion when Francesca's father, Bruno Mendozo, had first mentioned marriage to his daughter. Rocco's immediate impulse had been to recoil and renegotiate terms. It was true that he'd been contemplating marriage, but he'd definitely been going to select his own bride. But then he'd met Chessie and realised that she'd be perfect for his needs. In fact she'd been *exactly* the sort of woman he would have chosen himself. She'd dressed modestly, worn no make-up, and had obviously been not in the slightest bit interested in flirting. She'd lived her life in Sicily and she'd been a virgin. All his. And she had clearly been completely starstruck by him. What more could a man want from a wife?

Deciding that this was one business deal that was looking better by the minute, he'd agreed to the terms.

Looking at her now, dressed in a high-neck black top that drained the colour from her already pale cheeks, he wondered just what lay beneath that flawless skin and innocent expression. Was she missing her lover?

The thought of his wife with another man incited an attack of jealousy so fierce that Rocco wrestled with a sudden urge to splay her flat on the terrace and drive all thoughts of Carlo Mancini from her head. Later, he promised himself as he drained his glass. Later he'd take her to bed.

And she wouldn't be thinking of anyone but him.

Chessie poked listlessly at the food on her plate, her appetite gone. She couldn't believe she was back in Sicily with Rocco.

How had her life gone so horribly wrong? After all those years with her father, didn't she deserve her freedom?

After the short boat crossing, she'd spent the day lying on a huge bed, staring at the ceiling, too stressed to sleep, trying to summon up another escape plan. But so far she'd failed to come up with anything remotely workable.

It was too far to swim, and Rocco's staff were hardly likely to offer her a lift to the mainland.

She lifted her head and stared at the horizon. Beyond the

vine-covered terrace was a stretch of fine golden sand and then the sea. It was exquisitely beautiful, but she didn't notice. All she saw was the isolation. *There would be no escape from here.* The fire and resolve drained out of her, leaving her in a state of despair.

She had to get back to the mainland.

Staring at her plate again, she knew Rocco was watching her.

She could *feel* him looking at her with those dark, dangerous eyes. *Those stormy, passionate eyes that reflected the bad boy that he was.* One look from those eyes was enough to persuade the most virtuous of women to think extremely bad thoughts.

And she didn't want him in her thoughts at all.

She didn't want to think about his reputation with women, or the fact that she was trapped here with him, and she certainly didn't want to think about that kiss on the boat.

The kiss had confused her, because at the time it had felt like everything even though she knew it had meant nothing. She wasn't the sort of woman that Rocco Castellani normally glanced at once, let alone twice. Suddenly she had a clear vision of the blonde-haired slender girl who'd been wrapped around him at their wedding. If that girl was an example of his usual taste in women then it was no wonder that he kept reaching for his wine, she thought miserably. Her body was so far from his idea of feminine beauty that he probably had to get himself drunk in order to carry out his promise of taking her to bed.

How had this happened?

How had she ended up married to Rocco Castellani?

She put her fork down and picked up her wine glass, her mind drifting back to the day her father had told her of his plans for her wedding...

* * *

'Well? Aren't you going to say anything?' Bruno Mendozo's voice was harsh and impatient. 'Are you mute?'

No, she was shocked.

Chessie stared hard at the floor, knowing better than to look her father in the eye. Cringing with embarrassment, she curled her toes inside her flat, practical shoes. *Oh, dear God, her father was going to try and buy her a husband.* And not any old husband, but Rocco Castellani. Could there be anything more humiliating?

She didn't need to think about the taunts of the girls who had attended her convent school to know that nature hadn't been kind to her. True, she had blue eyes, but her hair was the colour of a raven's wing and her body had carried on growing in every direction long after others had stopped. Fully aware of her own deficiencies, she didn't need to study herself in the mirror to know that she was about as far from Castellani's normal choice of woman as it was possible to be.

He'd turn her down, of course. Why wouldn't he? Why would a sophisticated businessman like Rocco Castellani ever agree to marriage with a girl like her? A girl who'd never been allowed to travel further than the village? And the most humiliating thing of all was that deep in her pocket, carefully folded so that no one would see it, was a worn picture of him. She'd cut it out of a newspaper a year earlier and hidden it under her pillow. It had been a foolish, childish thing to do, but Rocco had a face and body that had fuelled a million female fantasies. He was just so impossibly handsome. The stuff of dreams. And dreams were all she had, because her life was totally barren and empty.

He was her Mr Darcy, her Heathcliffe and her Mr Rochester all rolled into one.

A man no woman had ever held onto.

In a world that increasingly encouraged a man to get in touch with his feminine side, Rocco Castellani was unashamedly masculine.

But Chessie hadn't cared. In fact she'd been drawn by his raw masculinity, his dangerous reputation and his bold refusal to please anyone but himself. The wife of a man like that would travel and see the world, and she'd lain awake at night thinking about what it would be like to be desired by someone like him. But she was mature enough to know what it was about Rocco that really drew her, and it wasn't his wealth or his looks. It was his strength. Rocco Castellani was tough and powerful and entirely indifferent to the opinion of others. And he was the only man she'd ever met who had what it took to stand up to her father.

And now her father was telling her that he'd set her up for the most humiliating rejection of all. He was telling Castellani that he had to marry her. But she knew that no price her father paid would be enough to persuade a man like Rocco to spend his life with someone like her.

And his rejection would be the ultimate humiliation.

'Go and brush your hair,' her father ordered, his black eyes filled with contempt. 'He'll be here in the next five minutes and he wants to meet you.'

Chessie stared at her father in horror. Brush her hair? Rocco Castellani was a man who dated models and actresses. What difference was it going to make whether she brushed her hair? What she really needed was to lose six inches in height and two stone in weight in the space of the next five minutes.

With an anguished glance at her mother, who was silent as usual, Chessie slid out of the room and returned to her bedroom. She splashed her face in the bathroom, and was just reaching for a comb when she heard the throaty growl of a powerful car approaching the house.

Sneaking to the window, she watched with a mixture of resignation and fascination as a sleek black sports car came to a halt outside the house and Castellani stepped out of the driver's seat.

Il lupo, she thought weakly as the comb slipped through her fingers and fell to the floor. The wolf. Wasn't that what the business pages called him? He attacked failing companies and either broke them up or turned them, depending on which was likely to make him the most profit. He was a risk-taker: bold, ruthless and fearless.

And he was the most amazing-looking man she'd ever seen.

His hair was glossy black, and gleamed under the powerful Sicilian sun. A pair of dark glasses covered his eyes, but she knew that they'd be dark, too. He was over six foot in height and powerfully built, with a lithe, athletic body that was designed to meet the most extreme physical challenge, and he wore his masculinity as easily as he wore his clothes. No woman could look at him and not want.

And then there was her…

Turning to look at herself in the mirror, Chessie suppressed a groan. How was he going to react when he saw her? He was probably going to pass out with shock and laughter that anyone would even *suggest* that he should marry her.

Suddenly she wished her wardrobe were full of sexy clothes, like the ones she knew other girls wore when they went out, but everything she owned was shapeless and dark. Her father didn't allow her to wear anything that might attract attention to her full figure. There was only one word to describe her, and that was 'frump'.

Wondering whether she had time to start digging an escape

tunnel, she went downstairs with a feeling of dread, preparing herself for humiliation.

Rocco Castellani was talking to her father in Italian, and they broke off when she entered the room.

Her father introduced her, and Chessie stood in anguished silence, not knowing what on earth she could possibly say to redeem the situation. If Rocco Castellani had any sense, he'd run while he still could.

But he didn't run.

He stood there, legs planted firmly apart in a stance as confident as it was aggressively masculine. Finally he broke the silence. 'Your gardens are beautiful,' he observed, in a velvety tone that heated her insides to melting point. 'Perhaps Francesca could show me around?'

Her father frowned his disapproval of that suggestion. 'I'll arrange for someone to accompany you.'

'That won't be necessary.' Rocco looked up and there was steel under his smile. 'Your daughter will be safe with me.'

Safe. *Safe?* Chessie clamped her lips together to stop herself from screaming with frustration. She didn't want to be safe. She wanted to escape from the repressive confines of her narrow, small little world. She wanted to *live*. She wanted to discover the true meaning of the word passion. If Rocco Castellani felt even remotely tempted to make a serious pass at her then that was fine with her.

All the other girls she knew had started experimenting with boys and sex while still at school, and here was she at the ripe age of twenty-one, not even allowed to go for a walk with a man unless someone was watching! Rocco was going to think she was a schoolgirl, and what man in his right mind wanted to marry an awkward adolescent?

Perhaps her father had realised that, because he finally

agreed and they walked together in the garden. Rocco totally relaxed and at ease; herself dying in a thousand agonies of shyness and embarrassment. But, instead of appearing bored, Rocco went out of his way to show her kindness. He gently probed and questioned until finally she was forced to abandon her tortured silence and answer him.

And he made her laugh. Twice. Which felt amazing, because she couldn't remember the last time she'd actually found anything in her life worth laughing at.

It was the first of several meetings, and each time Rocco insisted that they spend time alone, and each time he made her smile. By their fourth meeting she'd decided that he was the nicest person she'd ever met, and by their fifth meeting she was in love with him.

All the same, on the day that he asked her to marry him she stared at the ground, painfully self-conscious, unable to believe she'd actually heard him correctly.

'You're asking me because it's what my father wants.'

'If you think that then you don't know me at all,' he said, in that slow, lazy drawl that always made her nerve-endings tingle. 'I've never in my life done anything to please anyone but myself. I'm congenitally selfish.' He slipped a hand under her chin and lifted her face so that she was forced to look at him.

Chessie felt her insides tumble. He was asking her to marry him because it was what *he* wanted? 'I'm not the right sort of woman to be your wife.'

'You're *exactly* the right sort of woman to be my wife. If you weren't then we wouldn't be having this conversation now.'

She looked at him with disbelief. Rocco Castellani seriously wanted to marry her? 'Why?'

The look on his face indicated that he wasn't accustomed to explaining himself. 'Because we can have a good marriage,' he said, with arrogant self-assurance. 'We make each other laugh, and you are everything I want in a wife.'

She wanted to pinch herself and beat herself with sticks, just to see whether she'd wake up from the dream. She was the girl everyone at the convent had laughed at. She was frumpy and awkward. And yet this god among men had chosen her. *Rocco Castellani.* Suddenly she wanted to drag him into the middle of the village, just so that she could tell everyone and show him off.

'Francesca?' There was amusement in his tone. 'I'm waiting for an answer. Is it yes?'

An answer? He wanted her answer? Since when had a man ever cared about her opinion on anything? 'Yes,' she replied in a shaky voice. 'Yes, of course.' How could she contemplate a different answer? Suddenly the world seemed accessible. With him she could lead the sort of life that had only ever been in her dreams.

And they'd be happy.

No more agonising loneliness.

No more isolation.

She was finally going to *live*.

Chessie brought herself back to the present and realised that Rocco was still watching her. She gave up on the plate of food in front of her. Somehow just being with him had wiped out her appetite.

Her stomach churned and flipped in a way that she didn't recognise.

'Eat something.' He leaned forward and topped up her glass. 'Starving yourself isn't going to solve any of your problems.'

Neither was putting on any more weight. Painfully conscious that she was already several stone heavier than the woman he'd danced with at their wedding, she once again wished she were flat-chested. She wore baggy tops in dark colours, but still it wasn't possible to entirely conceal her shape.

'I'm really not hungry.'' She cast a sideways glance towards the villa, but there was no sign of the staff. 'I need to know where my mother is. Will you find her for me?'

'What makes you think I would I be able to do that?'

'You're Sicilian. You have influence, I know you do. You could find her if you wanted to.'

He helped himself to more wine. 'She should have stayed in the family home, mourning your father.'

'Don't *ever* judge my mother.' Forgetting her churning stomach, Chessie rose to her feet, her legs shaking. 'If you knew what she had put up with for all those years, you'd recommend her for a sainthood.'

Rocco's eyes lingered thoughtfully on her face. 'I'm starting to gain the impression that your father wasn't the easiest man to live with. Sit down, Francesca. Tension at the meal table gives me indigestion.'

She remained standing, her fingers gripping the table, her cheeks pink from the wine. 'You can't just—'

'Chessie.' His voice was level. 'Sit down.'

She sat, her heart thumping at his more informal use of her name. It was the first time he'd called her anything other than Francesca, and on his lips the shortened version of her name sounded—intimate?

'Do you get a thrill out of ordering me around?' There was a long silence and his eyes held hers. A powerful bolt of electricity stabbed through her body.

'I fully intend to show you what gives me a thrill as soon as I've finished my dinner,' he informed her in a silky tone, and she sank further into her seat.

'If you're talking about sex again then you ought to know that I have absolutely no desire to go to bed with you.'

He smiled. 'Of course you do. You're desperate to go to bed with me, but you're still sulking about Lorna. You can relax. I'm not with her any more. That relationship is over.'

Chessie gasped at his monumental lack of tact. 'And that's supposed to make me feel better?'

'Why wouldn't it? My relationship with Lorna was purely physical, and it's finished. Before our wedding.' Clearly believing that those facts made everything all right, he gave a careless shrug. 'So you really have no need to be jealous.'

'I keep telling you that I'm not jealous. I just don't like you!' She shook her head in disbelief. 'You say that your relationship was purely physical, but is it ever more than that for you? Do you ever actually *like* the women that you have affairs with?'

'Of course.'

'Have you ever been in love?'

Rocco muttered something in Italian that she didn't catch. Then he leaned forward, a slightly mocking gleam in his eyes. 'Grow up,' he advised, in a silky tone. 'You're in the real world now. Relationships between adults are complex and are carried out on many levels.'

'From what I can see, yours are carried out on only the one level,' Chessie muttered. 'And that's horizontal.'

Rocco lifted a hand in a dismissive gesture. 'And what's wrong with that? We both know you've done exactly the same thing, so stop acting like an outraged virgin. From this point onwards the past is forgotten.'

Suddenly she wished she hadn't told that lie about Carlo, but at the time she'd seriously believed that he'd reject her if he thought she'd been with another man. 'I don't find you attractive and I have no desire to go to bed with you.'

He reached for his glass, his expression amused. 'Fifteen seconds,' he said softly, raising the glass in a silent salute. 'That's all I need to make you change your mind. Possibly less.' His gaze dropped to her mouth and she felt a burning heat rush into her pelvis.

'Maybe I'm going to be the first woman to reject you. Did that thought ever occur to you?'

'No.'

She wished he'd stop looking at her mouth. Nervous and unsettled, she reached for her wine glass. Didn't people drink when they needed courage? Well, she needed a mountain of the stuff. She sipped cautiously, and then sipped again, pleasantly surprised by the flavour and the scent. Several mouthfuls later, her head started to swim. 'This tastes really good.'

'You're not supposed to drink the entire glass in one mouthful.'

'I'm thirsty.' She drained the glass. 'Is there any more?'

'Not until you've eaten some food.' Rocco slid the bottle out of her reach and she frowned at him, wondering why everything suddenly seemed fuzzy.

'Stop bossing me around.'

'Then stop acting like a child,' he advised, and she looked away, unable to stand his scrutiny any longer.

'Stop studying me. You'd drink too if you were in my position.'

'And what position is that?'

Should she confess that the thought of taking her clothes off in front of him made her want to die of embarrassment? No. Wasn't a lack of confidence supposed to be unattractive? Well, she was unattractive enough already, without adding to her problems. 'This isn't exactly a relaxed situation, is it?' she mumbled, letting her hand fall from the glass. Suddenly she felt exhausted. The stress of the flight, being met by Rocco, the discovery that her mother had left Sicily. It was all too much. 'I'm really tired. Am I allowed to go to bed?'

There was a brief silence while he studied her. 'This is your home,' he said evenly. 'You do as you please.'

Did he really expect her to believe that? She looked at him suspiciously, feeling suddenly dizzy. 'You mean, as long as it's something you approve of?'

'Of course.' He gave a faint smile and rose to his feet. 'Fortunately, going to bed is something that meets with my approval. I'll show you the bedroom.'

'I know where the bedroom is.'

'Today you rested in one of the guest rooms. Tonight you sleep in our bed.'

He guided her through the palatial villa, up a wide curving staircase and into a huge, airy bedroom. White filmy curtains floated in front of glass doors that opened onto a terrace.

'Oh—this is lovely.' Her legs feeling ridiculously heavy, Chessie wandered outside and swayed suddenly. 'My head feels sort of swimmy. It must be the wine.'

'You only drank one glassful.'

'Well, that's one glassful more than I've drunk in the rest of my life,' she slurred, and gave a sigh of relief as he swept her into his arms with a muttered imprecation. 'Thank you. That's so much better than walking.'

Her head swam as he laid her on the bed, and she opened her eyes and stared up at his bronzed, handsome face, noticing the firm lines of disapproval around his mouth.

'You're probably worried that you've married an alcoholic,' she mumbled sleepily as she rolled onto her side. 'But don't worry about it. Tonight is actually the first time I've ever touched alcohol, and the way my head is feeling now, it's definitely going to be the last.'

'The first time?' His voice was loaded with disbelief, and she gave a soft smile and closed her eyes, the world still spinning.

'Mmm. My father didn't approve of women drinking. Actually, he didn't approve of women at all—other than the ones he cheated on my mother with. A bit like you, really.' The pillow was incredibly soft. 'This is sooo comfortable. Night-night.'

Pacing the terrace outside the bedroom, Rocco tried to contain his mounting frustration.

She'd had one glass of wine and she was asleep on the bed.

Just where exactly had he gone wrong?

Francesca Mendozo should have been the perfect wife.

When he'd first met her, she'd been discreet and painfully well mannered. She had been gentle, compliant, and she'd looked at him with a flattering degree of admiration. In fact she'd been so visibly amazed at his proposal of marriage that Rocco had been entirely sure that his choice of wife was nothing short of perfect. She was sweet, and the excitement she'd shown when he'd kissed her had been pleasantly surprising. Recalling the unexpected thud of lust that had overtaken him during that one steamy encounter in the garden, Rocco frowned. He'd always suspected that his new bride had hidden passions.

He just hadn't expected her to display them to another man.

Rocco paced back across the terrace. Normally he prided himself on his level of self-restraint, but since his bride had reappeared on the scene he had fast been discovering that his threshold for explosion was lower than he'd thought.

He was fighting a continuous battle with a vicious jealousy that tormented his every waking moment. And he didn't want to feel like this. *He of all people should be aware of the destructive nature of that particular emotion.* The fact that she was no longer a virgin was irrelevant to their future.

He needed to put it behind him.

The fact that she was far from being the sweet-natured, easy-going girl he'd thought he'd married, and that she was proving more of a challenge to handle than his most difficult takeover bid, shouldn't matter.

But, however hard he tried, he couldn't ignore the fact that since her disappearance she appeared to be an entirely changed personality. In fact he was fast coming to the conclusion that Chessie was very possibly the most complex and contradictory woman he'd ever met.

One moment she was yelling at him in a storming temper, displaying all the characteristic signs of female jealousy, the next she was curled up on the bed in a ball, more child than woman.

And not once had she flirted with him or tried to please him in any way.

Rocco let out a long breath and jabbed his fingers through his hair, wondering why women couldn't be more straightforward.

None of this was turning out the way he'd planned.

When he'd made the decision that it was time to turn his attention to creating a family, he hadn't realised how complex and time-consuming the project would be. It should have been easy. Given the number of women who had dropped him hopeful hints about being on the receiving end of a proposal of marriage, he'd had no clue that the process would be anything other than entirely simple.

But handling Chessie was proving to be anything but simple, and he had absolutely no doubt that, given the chance, she'd be on the run again.

It was all about ego, he reminded himself. Despite her traditional Sicilian upbringing, Chessie was clearly super-sensitive about competition. Seeing Lorna at the wedding had dented her pride.

Resigning himself to the fact that marriage was clearly nowhere near as straightforward as he'd anticipated, Rocco lined up the facts and analysed them, treating the current problem in the same way that he treated any problem. He looked for solutions.

Like any complicated project, his marriage was going to need his personal care and attention—for the immediate term at least. But he had no doubt that if he concentrated his mind he would have his new wife eating out of his hand after just a couple of nights.

Checking his watch, he took the steps down from the terrace and strode over to the part of the villa that he'd had converted into a suite of offices.

The night was still young and his bride was asleep.

He might as well make a few calls to New York and see how the deal was progressing—to ensure that when his wife awoke he could devote his full attention to her.

CHAPTER FOUR

CHESSIE woke with a pounding headache and a spotlight glaring into her face. 'Oh, please will someone turn that light off,' she groaned, rolling onto her stomach and burying her face in the pillow.

'It's the sun,' came a cool, male voice from right beside her, and suddenly she was aware that the sheet was somewhere round her ankles. Cool air washed over her skin, and she realised that she was wearing only her underwear.

With a gasp of embarrassment she grabbed at the sheet and pulled it upwards, but it tangled in her legs, and it took several strong yanks on her part before she finally managed to cover herself to her satisfaction.

'What happened to my clothes?'

'I removed them five seconds after you fell unconscious,' Rocco drawled in a mocking tone. 'I have to confess that alcohol makes you a less than stimulating dinner companion. Tonight, remind me to give you water.'

Still struggling with the disturbing knowledge that he'd undressed her, Chessie sat up, clutching the sheet to her chin. 'It wasn't the alcohol. It was just lack of sleep. I was tired.' She stared at him, her eyes suddenly wide as she watched him remove his tie with a few careless movements of his long fingers. 'It's morning. Why are you undressing?'

'Because I haven't been to bed yet, and I don't intend to come to bed with you while wearing a suit.' He dropped the tie over the back of the nearest chair and shrugged off his jacket.

'Come to bed with me…' She clutched the sheet even tighter. 'We can't have sex now. It's daylight.'

The careless lift of his broad shoulders indicated that he considered that fact to be entirely irrelevant. 'I've been tied up in meetings all night, otherwise I would have been lying by your side, waiting for you to wake up. I've never been wedded to the idea that sex can only take place in darkness.' He removed his watch and placed it on the nearest table, then slowly undid the buttons on his shirt. 'Daylight works for me.'

'When it comes to sex, I suppose just about anything works for you,' she mumbled, horrified at the thought of him making love to her in broad daylight. It was her worst nightmare. Still clutching the sheet against her breasts, Chessie skidded back in the bed so fast that she almost bounced off the headboard. 'Look, we're really not doing this.'

'If you're worried about staying faithful to your lover, then I can assure you that after today you won't even remember his name,' Rocco informed her with characteristic confidence as he dropped the shirt and reached for the zip of his trousers.

Chessie averted her eyes, her cheeks scarlet. She'd never seen a male stripper before, but she was sure that Rocco would be up there with the best. Undressing in front of an audience clearly wasn't something that disturbed him in the slightest. But if she'd had a body like his, maybe she'd have been equally relaxed about revealing it.

She was unable to stop herself sneaking another look.

Dark hairs formed a shadow across his bronzed chest,

shading perfect musculature. He was all hard lines and powerful masculinity, and she couldn't help comparing him with the pictures of Renaissance sculptures she'd seen in books. A Michaelangelo or a Donatello, designed to capture the strength and muscular perfection of the male form. Only Rocco was no god cast in bronze. He was flesh and blood and very much alive.

As the zip descended she saw that the dark hairs trailed downwards, leading the eye to the significant bulge of masculinity that pressed against his silk boxer shorts.

Chessie gave a gulp and looked away quickly. This was definitely the point where she was supposed to tell him again that she hadn't actually slept with Carlo. To pretend to be experienced in bed was just asking for trouble, given her complete lack of knowledge in that direction.

But to confess to being a virgin would be to admit that no one had ever found her remotely desirable before now, and she just couldn't bring herself to say that aloud. It was obvious from the fact that he'd invited his mistress to their wedding that he didn't find her particularly desirable either, and she had no intention of reminding him of her deficiencies.

Surely she'd be able to pretend that she'd done it all before?

His boxer shorts slid to the floor and she suddenly found her gaze riveted to her first sight of an aroused male. Her heart flipped and her anxiety levels soared.

'Are you going to let go of that sheet?' He joined her on the bed and firmly prised the sheet from her lethal grip.

She spotted the loose black top she'd worn the night before lying on the floor, and wriggled across the bed to make a grab for it.

'What are you doing?' Lean, bronzed hands grabbed her around the waist and hauled her back into the centre of the bed, ignoring her quest for modesty. 'You're not going to need that.'

'I was just going to put my top on.'

'What would be the point of that?' he asked softly, stroking her tangled hair away from her face in a supremely confident gesture. 'When I'd only have to take it off again?'

'Listen—' her voice was shaky '—it's time to stop fooling around. I'm not the sort of woman you normally sleep with. We both know that.' He was probably going to take one look at her and lose his erection, she thought miserably, as she slunk as far under the sheet as she possibly could.

'Stop talking about other women.' A note of exasperation in his voice, he prised the sheet away from her hands for a second time and pushed it out of reach. 'I'm with you now, and that's all that matters.'

Aware that his gaze had dropped to her breasts, Chessie felt hot, burning colour flood into her cheeks. If intense embarrassment could have shrunk her breasts then her chest would have been flat.

The silence seemed to extend for ever, and all the fight went out of her while she waited for him to say something derogatory. 'Stop looking at me. I know I've got the wrong sort of body,' she mumbled finally, trying to wriggle away from him.

He held her firmly, a strange look in his dark eyes. 'The wrong sort of body? What's that supposed to mean?'

Was he going to make her spell it out? 'We've already established that I don't look anything like those models you usually date. I'm fat.'

'*Not* fat,' he assured her in husky tones, pushing her gently onto her back and sliding a leisurely hand over the soft curve of her abdomen. 'You have exactly the *right* sort of body. It's perfect.'

Perfect? Chessie opened her mouth to argue with him, but he chose that precise moment to close his mouth over her right nipple. She gave a soft gasp, her body arching off the bed in an involuntary movement as hot flames of lust shot through her. His tongue flicked and teased, and the sensations intensified to almost unbearable proportions. She gave a low moan, her eyes drifting shut as her whole body was racked by an excitement so powerful that she dug her nails into the smooth skin of his bronzed shoulder.

'We shouldn't be doing this—'

'We're married,' he purred. 'And we should have done this six months ago.'

He turned his attention to her other breast, and the insistent throb between her legs became an almost agonising ache. Chessie shifted against the sheets in an attempt to ease the growing tension inside her, but he spread his hand over her shifting pelvis and held her still.

'Rocco—' in the grip of feelings that she didn't recognise, she gasped his name, and he gave a low laugh and covered her body with his in a lithe, powerful movement that left no doubt as to who was in control.

'You like that, no?' He made a rough sound and brought his mouth down on hers, at the same time sliding his hand underneath her and cupping the rounded curve of her bottom. 'You feel fantastic. I knew from the first moment I saw you that sex with you was going to be incredible.'

He had? He'd really thought that? She tried to hold onto that thought, but the erotic stroke of his tongue inside her mouth and the touch of his skilful fingers sent her body surging at breakneck speed along a road of sensual discovery.

Suddenly there was nothing in her world but the physical reaction of her body. Her pelvis throbbed and ached, seeking a deeper satisfaction, and she was dimly aware of the friction of rough, male body hair against sensitive female skin. He was all hard, strong muscle against her soft, rounded curves. Then he shifted slightly and she felt his hand move, felt the slide of his fingers exploring her intimately.

'Oh—' it was the first time any man had touched her there, but his touch was so sure and confident that her resistance evaporated in an instant. Unfamiliar sensations racked her body, and she cried out in shock, instinctively tried to move her hips, but he anchored her with the weight of his body and continued to kiss her until her world was spinning and indistinct.

'Does that feel good, *cara*?' The soft purr of his voice against her ear barely registered against the practised skill of his fingers. 'Do you like that?'

'It feels amazing and I think I want—I need you to— Rocco—' She sobbed his name and dug her nails into the smooth, bronzed skin of his shoulder, and he gave a husky laugh that resonated with masculine satisfaction.

'Any time you want me to stop you only have to say so.'

'Stop? No, don't stop,' she gasped against his mouth, lifting her hips in a frantic attempt to relieve the almost unbearable building of tension.

'What is it you want, tesoro? This?'

With single-minded purpose he shifted her position slightly, pushed her thighs apart, and entered her with a decisive masculine thrust.

The size and power of him stole the breath from her body, and as he slid an arm under her hips and thrust deeper she gave a murmur of protest.

Instantly he stilled, tension visible in his handsome face as he looked down at her. 'I'm hurting you?'

Afraid to move in case it made the pain worse, she lay rigid, staring up at him. 'What makes you say that?'

There was a gentle humour in his eyes as he stroked her tangled hair away from her face with a surprisingly light touch. 'Possibly the fact that your nails are drawing blood from my shoulder?'

'Oh—' she let her hands fall to her sides. 'Sorry.'

'Has anyone ever told you that you're crazily mixed up?' His expression thoughtful, he studied her for a moment, and then his hand slid into her hair and he lowered his head and took her mouth. 'Kiss me,' he urged softly against her lips, his voice hoarse with restrained passion. 'Kiss me, *tesoro*, and everything will be all right. Trust me.'

Feeling the rough scrape of male stubble over the sensitive skin of her face, she opened her mouth under the demanding pressure of his and gave a low moan as he took control. His kiss was slow and purposeful, designed to arouse and excite, and she squirmed against him as her insides turned to liquid and drove coherent thought from her head.

She forgot that there'd ever been pain, because suddenly her body was consumed by pleasure.

He withdrew slightly and entered her again, and this time all she felt was the most wickedly delicious sensation of fullness and male possession. She felt his hands on her hips, felt him subtly alter her position, then surge inside her with sufficient care and control for her sudden gasp to this time be one of ecstasy. Her whole body was on fire, burning up with a desire that she hadn't even known existed, and when Rocco lifted her, plunging deeper still into her silken core, she gave a sob of desperation, utterly consumed by the strength and skill of his possession.

Excitement flowed through her in hot, greedy waves, and

she gasped his name and arched into him, moving her hips to the rhythm he'd set.

Sensations overwhelmed her body—sensations that she didn't recognize—and she gave a sob of disbelief as she shot into a climax so breathtakingly intense that her world suddenly splintered apart and her body throbbed around the powerful thrust of his. The pulse of her body went on and on, and then she heard his harsh groan and felt the sudden increase in masculine thrust as the strength of her orgasm drove him into his own.

Eventually the storm eased, and Chessie lay with her eyes closed, feeling the intimate throb of his body joined with hers, shocked and dazed by what had happened to her. *She hadn't known.* Even in her wildest dreams she hadn't been able to imagine that it would be like that. *It was so much more than a physical experience. It was an overwhelming connection and a closeness that couldn't possibly be expressed by words.* And the closeness astonished her.

She was used to being solitary.

All her life she'd been a private person. Her father had held her at a distance and discouraged friendships. Unbearably lonely, her relationships had been with books, her friends the characters living inside them.

But this—she felt the warm, sluggish afterglow of incredible sex and gave a faint smile—this was the real thing. No amount of fictional description had prepared her for the overpowering satisfaction that came with real human intimacy. *Man-woman intimacy.*

It was only now, with her body trembling under his, that she knew what it was like to truly share. *To give all of herself to another person.*

She lay still underneath him, reluctant to move, wanting

desperately to prolong the perfection of the moment. Trapped by the weight and power of his body, she listened as his breathing slowed, felt the roughness of his chest brush the smooth silk of her skin as he moved. Suddenly the harshness of real life seemed like a distant place. Held like this, her body warm and throbbing with unfamiliar sensations, she suddenly couldn't remember why she'd wanted a divorce. She forgot why she'd wanted her freedom so badly. *Why would she want anything more than this? What more was there?*

When he eased out of her and rolled onto his back she wanted to hold onto him and beg him never to move, but her tongue wouldn't form the words. She had no idea how to behave after such a cataclysmic assault on her senses. Had he felt it too? *Had it affected him the same way?* Unable to resist the temptation to look at him, she turned her head and felt everything inside her dissolve into liquid longing.

He was indecently handsome.

Unable to help herself, she let her hungry gaze move over the hard, masculine planes of his profile and linger on the strong lines of his darkened jaw.

As if sensing her scrutiny, he turned to look at her. 'Don't *ever* let me think that you slept with another man again.' His voice had a hard edge, and hinted at a boiling cauldron of emotions fiercely suppressed. 'I could have killed him.'

Basking in the aftermath of sexual perfection, braced to hear something suitably romantic, Chessie felt the warm, soft feeling evaporate inside her. 'Wh-what are you talking about?'

'Mancini.' Rocco lay on his back. He made no attempt to cover himself, totally unselfconscious about his nudity. 'Either he's useless as a lover, or you were lying to me about what happened. Until this morning you were a virgin.'

Her expectations of hearing soft, romantic words well and

truly crushed, Chessie felt the colour flood into her cheeks. This wasn't the conversation they should be having. 'I tried to tell you the truth—'

'But only after you'd first told me a lie. Just for the record, telling your Sicilian husband that you're sleeping with another man is a dangerous game, *tesoro*. Don't risk it again.' He rolled onto his side and looked down at her, the fire in his eyes fading to slumberous satisfaction. 'But I'm pleased you were a virgin. *Extremely* pleased. In the circumstances, I might just forgive you for running away.'

Forgive *her*?

Chessie lay in bemused silence, searching those stormy molten eyes for some hint of gentleness. *Something that reflected the deep emotional intensity of their lovemaking.* They'd just shared something impossibly intimate. Where were the words of affection that were supposed to follow? 'Is that all you have to say? Is that all you care about? My virginity?'

'Is that so surprising?' His satisfied smile was all male, and he slid a bronzed hand over the curve of her hip in a sensual gesture. 'You're my wife, and I've never been any good at sharing. I was trying to be relaxed about it, but I have to confess that it was an uphill struggle.'

Her body responded instantly to his touch and she felt a warm, heavy feeling spread across her pelvis. 'You're unbearably possessive.'

'Thank you.' He moved his hand, sprang out of bed, and prowled towards the bathroom, gloriously naked and totally indifferent to the fact. 'Best remember that before you accept any more lifts from strangers.'

She lay still for a moment, thrown by the fact that he'd taken her criticism as a compliment, trying to ignore the dangerous throb in her body. Then disappointment rose inside her, swamping her fledgling happiness.

This was her first sexual experience and he knew it. And had he said one single romantic thing to her? Had he uttered one gentle word? No. It was obvious that the entire episode just been about his need to make her his. So much for closeness and intimacy. And so much for her ego. He probably hadn't even noticed her body. For him it had been about nothing more than possession.

Unbelievably crushed, Chessie lay still.

Then she felt determination grow inside her—a determination that had been nurtured by her six months away from her father. No man was going to treat her badly again.

She slid off the bed and made a grab for his discarded shirt. Her hands shaking, she pushed her arms into the sleeves and gathered it around her. Then she followed him into the bathroom, walking through the door just in time to see him hit a button on the wall that sent jets of water pouring onto the tiled floor.

'I want to talk to you.'

'Talking after sex is an overrated pastime,' he drawled as he reached for a towel. 'I prefer just to enjoy the physical.'

'Well, that's pretty obvious.' The reminder that none of the feelings she was experiencing were new to him simply increased her misery. 'I think your bedroom technique needs work.'

He turned, treating her to an uninterrupted view of his gloriously male body. Suddenly her fingers itched with the need to draw him, and she took an involuntary step backwards, almost blinded by his physical perfection. She'd sketch him in pencil, using strong, bold strokes... She looked away, knowing instinctively that no artist, not even Michelangelo or Da Vinci, would be able to do justice to the masculine power of his body. A drawing would always be two-dimensional, and even a sculpture wouldn't be able to faithfully reproduce the glossy curves of hard, strong muscle.

Ominously still, Rocco watched her for a long moment, his dark eyes glittering with incredulous disbelief. '*What* did you say?'

She swallowed hard, trying not to be intimidated by the power and strength of his physique. 'I said that your bedroom technique needs work.'

'You've just had an incredible orgasm—I suspect the first of your life. I left you limp and exhausted on the bed.' His voice was low and deadly, his eyes glinting dangerously. 'Just what exactly needs work?' He prowled over to her, and she gave a soft gasp and averted her eyes from the curling dark hairs that shaded his broad chest.

He was too close.

'It wasn't the sex, it was afterwards,' she muttered, her cheeks burning hot as fire as she concentrated on the tiles. 'You didn't say anything—nice.'

'*Nice?*' He sounded genuinely confused. 'What do you mean by nice?'

'You didn't say anything personal. And if you didn't find me attractive then it's your own fault. I warned you not to do it in daylight,' she said, and there was a long silence.

'What does daylight have to do with anything?'

She bit her lip. 'If you'd waited until dark, you wouldn't have been able to see my body.'

'Which is precisely why I chose full sunlight,' he responded in a silky tone, sliding a hand under her chin and forcing her to look at him. 'Why wouldn't I want to see your body?'

Did he need her to spell it out? 'I'm not your usual type. I thought perhaps you—'

He interrupted her. 'What would you change about your body?' He spoke in his usual tone of command. 'Tell me. I want to know.'

'Oh—well, that's obvious.' She tried to look away from him, but his fingers held her fast, preventing her from moving. 'I'd have smaller everything. Smaller boobs, smaller hips, shorter legs—'

'Then it's fortunate for me that you're not in a position to alter what nature has given you.' He released her chin, caught the hem of his shirt and pulled it upwards, resisting her feeble attempt to stop him. 'Your body is perfect, *tesoro*. I would change nothing except your continued desire to cover it up.'

Perfect? He'd said that once before, and she hadn't believed him then, either. Instinctively she tried to shield herself with her arms, but he gave a soft laugh and took her wrists, forcing her to loop her arms round his neck.

'Don't,' she whispered. 'You can't possibly like my body.'

'You need further proof?' Sliding his hands around her waist, he hauled her against him in a decisive movement, and she felt the hard thrust of his erection pressing against her.

Her gasp of shock was muffled by the demanding pressure of his kiss.

'Convinced yet, *angelo mio*?'

Dizzy from the unexpected assault on her senses, she tried to remember what their conversation had been about. 'So if you find me attractive then why did you leap out of bed so suddenly?'

'Because I can't be in bed with you and not make love.' He gave a slow, sexy smile and stroked her hair away from her face. 'And it is too soon for that. I don't want to hurt you, so I decided to take a long, cold shower as an alternative.'

'Oh.' Her eyes flitted to the shower and she noticed the distinct absence of steam. He was taking a cold shower?

When he'd left the bed so quickly he'd been thinking of *her*? In a *good* way?

'And now I have a question for you,' he said softly, sliding a hand over the soft curve of her bottom with almost arrogant assurance. 'I want to know exactly who made you think you are fat?'

'I don't know.' She gave an embarrassed shrug. 'The girls at school. My father. Myself, looking in the mirror. Everyone, I suppose.'

He frowned sharply. 'Your own father knocked your confidence?'

'I think it would be more accurate to say that he attacked it with a cricket bat,' she said flatly, and then realised that she'd probably said too much. She frowned slightly, astounded by her own behaviour. *After twenty-one years of keeping her mouth clamped shut, she suddenly seemed to be speaking her mind at every possible opportunity.*

His eyes rested on her face, his expression thoughtful. 'I see. Well, your father was wrong, and I never want to hear you speak of yourself like that again. Your body is perfect in every way. There is absolutely nothing I would change.'

Softened by the compliment, and the unexpected gentleness in his eyes, she let her hands trail downwards, loving the satiny strength of his shoulders. 'Nothing? You really mean that?'

'Absolutely.' He murmured the words against her mouth. 'You are everything I want and I'm going to prove it to you. Again and again, *tesoro*.'

And he did.

The next two weeks passed in a blur of sexual ecstasy, and it became increasingly obvious to her that Rocco just couldn't leave her alone. All night, every night, he made love to her, ignoring her inhibitions and her insecurities, taking such obvious pleasure in her body that it was impossible for her to feel anything other than completely desired. And it felt fantastic.

And if he wasn't exactly affectionate, he was extremely complimentary about her body, and she told herself that it was a start. Rocco clearly wasn't used to expressing his feelings, and she had some sympathy with that because neither was she.

They'd learn, she told herself as she lay in a satisfied stupor two weeks after she'd arrived back in Sicily. Together, they'd learn.

She knew he cared about her because he showed her that he did, and for the first time in her life she felt good about herself.

She felt attractive.

She felt sexy.

She felt like a woman.

When it came to sexual Olympics, Rocco definitely took the gold medal. His energy levels and stamina were nothing short of awesome.

Each day now followed the same pattern. He'd work in the suite of offices that took up one wing of the spacious villa, and then he'd spend the entire night making love to her before rising at dawn to begin another working day. His schedule was punishing, and when he ate and slept she had absolutely no idea. A small, nagging part of her wished he'd spend more daylight hours with her—*wished that they shared more than mind-blowing sex*—but then she reminded herself that he was a billionaire, and billionaires didn't make their money by lounging around all day, even if they *were* newly married.

On more than one occasion it crossed her mind to wonder *why* a man so wealthy continued to be so driven in his working habits, but she didn't have the opportunity to ask because their relationship didn't include time for conversation. And that was fine, she told herself. Didn't lots of relationships begin life focused on sex and then move on to deeper, more lasting emotions?

And as for her own feelings—being with him was the first real adventure she'd had in her life. Rocco made her feel feminine and desirable, and he knew things about her body that came as a complete surprise to her.

Her burning desire for freedom had retreated into the recesses of her mind, and her entire focus was their relationship.

Every night he strolled into their bedroom like a warrior claiming the spoils of battle, and every night her resolution that this was the night they were just going to cuddle up and talk lasted less than ten seconds.

Their relationship was basic and primitive, but it was also sensitive and caring, and she no longer had any doubts that he found her attractive. In fact she was becoming increasingly convinced that he actually *liked* her. Why else would he spend hour after hour making love to her? He couldn't leave her alone, and she just loved the fact that he clearly found her so addictive.

It was only a matter of time before the closeness spread into other parts of their lives, she assured herself. He'd take her with him on business trips abroad; they'd travel and they'd spend time exploring together.

Rolling onto her back and feeling the faint protest of her aching body, Chessie gave a satisfied feminine smile. He might not have said that he loved her, but he *definitely* loved her body, which was a start. Over and over again he'd tell her that she was perfect.

Perfect.

She rolled the word around in her head and smiled a satisfied. The fact that he just couldn't stop having sex with her delighted her. He made love to her repeatedly, night after night, telling her that he found her completely irresistible, and for the first time in her life she was starting to feel confident about the way she looked.

And he hadn't spent a single night away from her since they'd arrived on the island, she reminded herself, hugging the knowledge to her like a warm blanket. Since he'd deposited her in his bed on that first night, he clearly hadn't felt the need to see other women.

In fact she was coming to the conclusion that she'd been wrong in thinking that he was like her father.

Entirely wrong.

It was true that Rocco was strong and tough, but he was also sensitive to her needs, and they were becoming closer with each passing night of passion. Had her father spent every night in her mother's bed? No. She knew for a fact that he hadn't.

Feeling confident that it was only a matter of time before Rocco found that he couldn't go a whole day without seeking out her company, Chessie slid out of bed, took a quick shower, and then dressed and reached for her bag.

She'd taken to spending her days on the beach, catching up on sleep and indulging in her secret hobby. Drawing. She no longer had to hide what she did, because Rocco had better things to do than rifle through her things as her father had habitually done. Most days she swam; sometimes she just lay there, drawing and dreaming of Rocco, thinking of the night ahead.

But today, as she settled herself on her rug on the sand, she felt ridiculously unsettled.

She missed Rocco.

Glancing at her watch, she realised that it was barely afternoon. Hours yet until he'd arrive in their bedroom.

Unless she went to see him. And why shouldn't she? Why should it always be Rocco who took the initiative?

Feeling incredibly daring, she gathered up her things and walked back to the villa, slowly plucking up the courage she needed to go and see him in the wing of the villa that he used as an office.

To her surprise, it was a hive of activity.

Four extremely pretty girls were clearly snowed under with work in a light, airy office, and beyond them, in a much larger glass-fronted room with a breathtaking view of the sea, was Rocco.

He was perched on the edge of his desk, cradling the telephone between his shoulder and his ear, in the middle of what was clearly a heated exchange. The perfect white of his rolled-up shirtsleeves contrasted with the bronze of his forearms, and the fluid, demonstrative gestures he made with his hand indicated his growing frustration at the direction of the conversation.

For a moment Chessie paused in the doorway, captivated by the width of his shoulders and the command in his voice as he issued a string of complex instructions down the phone. And then his eyes lifted and he saw her.

'I'll call you back.' He replaced the phone, cutting the connection without apology or visible sign of regret. His eyes were hard, his expression businesslike as he focused on her dishevelled appearance. 'Has something happened? Is something the matter?'

It was a reflection of their marriage, she acknowledged ruefully, that he would associate her presence with a problem. Apart from their physical relationship, they never spent time together. They never usually even saw each other during the day. But she was about to change all that. She was about to move their relationship to a different level—give him the nudge that he needed.

Suddenly she wished she hadn't come straight from the beach. She should have stopped to change. Not that her wardrobe was exactly extensive, but she was suddenly horribly conscious that her beach clothes were creased.

'Nothing's the matter.' How could anything be the matter when the incredible night they'd shared only hours earlier was still replaying in her head? 'I just wanted to see you. To talk.'

'Talk?' He repeated the word as if it were something foreign that he didn't recognize, and then he straightened and walked towards her. 'What about?'

He was so tall, she mused dreamily. Six foot two at least. *He was the only man who'd ever made her forget her own height.* With him she no longer felt like a displaced giraffe, and she had no need to hunch or wear flat shoes.

Chessie linked her hands together, wondering how to revive the intimacy that had enveloped them both during the previous night. She just wanted him to say something soft—something affectionate that would prove that he cared for her. *But he wasn't great at that,* she admitted with a faint frown. Rocco was more about action than words.

Realising that his staff were probably listening to every word, she glanced over her shoulder. 'Can we close the door?'

'I'm working, Chessie.'

Trying not to be discouraged by his businesslike tone, she reminded herself that he hadn't been expecting to see her, and probably still had his mind on his phone call. 'It's just that I wanted to talk to you. In private.'

He studied her face for a moment, and then the hardness of his gaze was replaced by something softer. The tension in the air was replaced by a sense of anticipation. He strolled the length of his office and slammed the door shut with the flat of his hand. 'We have privacy,' he announced in a silky tone. 'And I am looking forward to hearing what it is that you have to tell me.'

'You're not angry with me for disturbing you?'

'Some things are worth being disturbed for, and this is certainly one of them.' He walked back to her, a smile on his face, and she felt the warm flood of relief spread through her limbs. She'd been right to come. He *did* care for her. It was just that he wasn't used to being interrupted in the middle of his working day, and he obviously found it hard to express his feelings. Clearly he needed a little prompting.

'I wanted to talk to you. I couldn't wait until tonight.'

'That's understandable,' he purred, lowering his mouth to hers in a brief but lingering kiss. 'Why wait when you have something important to divulge? I'm glad you came.'

Suitably encouraged, Chessie smiled up at him. 'I want us to spend more time together.'

'Of course you do—and we will.' His own smile was indulgent. 'Family trips. Picnics. I sense that your own father was very strict with you and had very little to do with your upbringing. You needn't worry. I think it's very important for a boy to have a male role model, and I intend to be a very involved with my son right from the beginning.'

His son? She stared at him blankly. 'What are you talking about?'

'You are trying to tell me that you're pregnant. You needn't worry. I'm delighted by the news—and of course I've been expecting it.'

He thought she was *pregnant*? 'Wh-why would you be expecting me to be pregnant?'

'Why else have we made love all night, every night for the past two weeks if not to make you pregnant?' He gave a careless shrug. 'Creating a family is what our marriage is about. It's fantastic news. I'm really, really pleased, *tesora*. You're a clever girl.'

She gaped at him in disbelief, his words echoing in her head. A flashback to endless ecstatic sex suddenly careered through her mind. 'This past two weeks…' Her voice almost failed her, because a horrifying, alternative scenario that she hadn't previously contemplated was forming in her mind. 'You were trying to make me pregnant?'

'Of course.' His faint frown revealed that he considered her question superfluous. 'What else?'

What else? She wanted to ask him about passion and desire, but her mouth wouldn't form the words. Instead her brain sifted through the information at her disposal. 'Y-you told me my body was perfect.'

'And it *is* perfect. How could you doubt it?' He stood back from her, his eyes dropping to her full breasts and then moving lower still, to the curve of her hips. 'I've told you that over and over again. Everything about you is designed for motherhood. Your hips are perfectly curved—designed for bearing children.'

Designed for bearing children? He thought her body was perfect because *it was designed for bearing children?* Not because she was sexy and irresistible?

The fragile shoots of her confidence snapped, and for a moment she was so shocked she couldn't think, let alone speak.

'I need to sit down,' she croaked weakly, and instantly his arm came around her and he guided her to the squashy cream sofa in the corner of his office.

'Of course you do.' His tone was smooth and concerned. 'You need plenty of rest, and I'm very sympathetic. From now on I'll leave you alone at night. You can sleep.'

It was the last thing she'd wanted or expected to hear, and

she sat down on the sofa with a plop, her legs shaking too much to hold her. Her mouth was suddenly dry, and she had to lick her lips before she could form the words that needed to be said. 'You didn't come to bed every night because you found me attractive but because you wanted us to have a baby?' Slightly dazed, she mumbled the words almost to herself, as if by voicing the truth aloud she might be able to make sense of it. 'You didn't really like my body?'

'How many times do I have to say it? I think your body is perfect.'

'P-perfect for producing an heir,' she stammered, feeling the anger rise inside her. 'That's different to finding me attractive.'

'If I didn't find you attractive,' he drawled, 'I wouldn't have made love to you four times a night for the past few weeks.'

Five times a night, she thought to herself, but she was too stunned to correct him. 'And it didn't occur to you to discus it with me?'

'What is there to discuss?' He frowned. 'Pregnancy is a natural conclusion of marital sex.'

Marital sex? 'In the Middle Ages, maybe,' she said, hearing her voice rise and not bothering to do anything about it. 'But not now. Women have jobs, Nowadays women plan their families with their partners. They both decide when to have children and how many to have.'

'And so have we.' He gave a casual shrug. 'Given that you don't have a job, and we have no financial constraints, I'd say loads and straight away.'

'Oh, would you?' The shine in her eyes betrayed her growing outrage. 'And do *I* get any say at all in this?'

His glance was impatient. 'There are absolutely no reasons why we shouldn't have as many children as possible as *soon* as possible. You're young and healthy and you were born to be a mother. Why wait?'

Still coming to terms with the fact that his obsession with her body had nothing to do with lust and everything to do with his desire for a child, Chessie swallowed and tried to force her voice past the lump in her throat. 'Have you any idea how I feel right now? Any idea at all?'

'Blessed?' Obviously sensing that he was facing a problem that as yet remained beyond his grasp, Rocco was suddenly watchful. 'There are millions of women who would kill to be in your position.'

'There are also millions of women who would kill *you* for placing them in my position,' Chessie muttered through gritted teeth, her nails digging into her palms as she struggled to control her emotions. 'If I was the violent type, I think you'd be dead on the floor by now.'

'I'm sure that's just your hormones,' Rocco offered helpfully, and Chessie rose to her feet, so incensed that she was ready to thump him and take the consequences.

'You don't have a clue, do you? You just don't know what's going on in my head.'

'No man would ever be optimistic enough to pretend that he understands what's going on in a woman's head—especially when that woman happens to be pregnant,' Rocco assured her in his characteristically lazy drawl. 'And I don't believe in investing time in losing situations. We don't have to understand each other to be married.'

'But it would be a start, don't you think?' Chessie stared at him in helpless frustration. Not only did he know *nothing* about her, he didn't seem remotely interested in finding out. It was obvious that he believed that she was here to produce children. Nothing more. That was her job description.

'Did it ever occur to you that I might have plans that don't include children?'

His eyes narrowed. 'Such as what, precisely?'

'I want to travel, I want to live my life—*I want a job, Rocco.*' There. She'd said it, and suddenly her heart was beating so fast that she wondered whether she might faint. 'I want to work.'

His eyes were suddenly cold. 'Why would you possibly want to work when you have access to more money than you could ever need?'

'It isn't about the money. It's about self-esteem and enjoyment—about being like other people and—' *And she wanted to do something with art.* She broke off, her outburst quashed by the hardness of his eyes. 'I'm trying to make you understand.'

'Understand what? That my wife doesn't want children?'

'I'm not saying that I don't want them,' she said quickly. 'Just that I don't want them quite *yet.* I suppose I assumed it was something we'd talk about. Didn't it occur to you that there are other things I want to do first?'

'Why would it? I haven't been using any contraception and you haven't once protested,' he drawled, his eyes intent on her face. 'You're very pale, and obviously upset. You need more sleep than you've been getting. You're tired. I'll have a doctor flown in this afternoon to check you out, and I'll stop disturbing your nights.'

He wasn't listening to her. 'You mean, having managed to sow your seed, you no longer have to expend all your energy trying to make me pregnant?' Chessie said stiffly, still recovering from her sudden realization that they had used no contraception. 'Well, I hate to disappoint you, but there's no need to waste the doctor's time. I'm not pregnant. And I'm not hormonal, Rocco. I'm just really, *really* angry.'

He stilled. 'You're not pregnant?'

'*Not* pregnant.' She repeated the words slowly, so that there could be no misunderstanding. 'I'm not having your baby, so if that's really your aim then you still have some *serious* work to do. Perhaps you'd better make it six times a night, just to be sure?'

His eyes were suddenly cold. 'You disturbed my working day in order to tell me that you're *not* pregnant?'

'No, I *didn't* interrupt your working day to tell you that I'm not pregnant! The subject of pregnancy hadn't even crossed my mind until you brought it up! I didn't come here to tell you *anything*. I just wanted to—' She broke off, anger and frustration giving way to helpless misery. How could she possibly confess that she wanted to spend more time with him when he clearly didn't share the same emotion? She wanted to leap on him and hurt him for being so *incredibly* insensitive.

It was obvious that he didn't care for her at all, and the fact that for a while she'd really believed that he did made her want to sink through the floor with humiliation and self-loathing.

She'd done it again.

Been taken in by Rocco's fatal charm; made a fool of herself over him in the same way that dozens of other women had before her.

She'd believed that he was something he wasn't. *She'd believed that he'd cared.* The moment he'd taken her in his arms she'd started thinking love and romance, and he'd been thinking sex and babies.

Stupid, stupid, *stupid*.

Determined to leave the room before she embarrassed herself in front of him, Chessie scrambled to her feet. 'This is a pointless conversation. I need to go,' she muttered. 'No doubt I'll see you later, for another determined baby-making session.'

'Sarcasm doesn't suit you.' His hand closed over her shoulder and he turned her back to face him. 'You're not leaving until we reach a satisfactory conclusion.'

'This isn't a business deal, Rocco! And a "satisfactory conclusion" to you is just getting your own way. You railroad everyone who stands in your way, but you're not doing it with me!' Her heart thumping, she lifted her chin. 'I'm your wife, and we're supposed to be a team. I will not allow you to bully me.' She'd made that promise to herself, and she intended to keep it.

Rocco stared at her with mounting disbelief. 'I am *not* bullying you,' he ground out with raw emphasis. 'And we *are* a team.'

'How can we be a team when we never talk?' Oh, what the heck? She might as well tell him the truth. Tears smarting in her eyes, she lifted her chin and stared him in the eye. 'That was why I came here. To try to introduce something into our relationship apart from the physical. Do you realise that in the past two weeks we've hardly exchanged a single word? I wanted us to spend time together, which is something we never do—and I've just discovered why. You're not interested in talking. In fact you're obviously not interested in me at all. You say that you want a wife, but when have you spent a single minute with me?' She gave a short, humourless laugh. 'My role is simply to provide you with a son. You just want to make me pregnant—which explains why I never see you during the day and why you spend the entire night competing for the title of super-stud.'

Looking like a man trying to stand on shifting ground, Rocco ran a hand over the back of his neck. 'There's an element of truth in what you're saying, but you're twisting it to make it seem bad. I can see that you're upset—'

'Really? You can tell that just by looking?' Chessie tossed

her head angrily and her dark hair spilled down her back. 'Then you're more sensitive than appearances would suggest.' She went to stalk out of his office, but he caught her by the arm again, and swung her round so that she was forced to face him.

'I see you as the perfect mother for my children,' he growled, incredulity and frustration lighting his dark eyes. 'What bigger compliment is there for a woman?'

'Oh, let me see…' She blinked back the tears that threatened. 'Finding a woman irresistible, interesting, stimulating company—those would all be bigger compliments.'

'Not from where I'm standing.'

'Let me ask you something, Rocco—and I want you to give me an honest answer. Do you ever look at me and want to rip my clothes off and take me there and then just because you can't help yourself?'

'What sort of a question is that?'

'A perfectly reasonable one. Answer me, Rocco.' Her voice was hoarse and she stepped closer to him. 'Do you find me *sexy*?'

'This is *not* the sort of conversation I expect to have with my wife.' The chill was back in his eyes and she turned away, helpless with exasperation and so miserable she just wanted to lie down and sob.

'Forget it, Rocco.' Her voice was choked. 'It's a shame we didn't have this conversation earlier—because it's perfectly clear to me now that we both expect entirely different things from marriage. I'll leave you to get on with your work. It's clearly all you care about.'

CHAPTER FIVE

SHE didn't mean anything to him at all.

Nothing.

Chessie stuffed clothes into her bag, crying so hard that her head throbbed and her face was blotched.

It was just as well Rocco didn't want a sexy wife, she thought to herself as she fumbled for yet another tissue and blew her nose, because at the moment she was as far from sexy as it was possible to be.

And the worst thing was that it didn't even matter. Clearly she could have had the physical attributes of an oil tanker and he wouldn't have cared, providing she gave him a son.

She'd been flattering herself that he found her irresistible, and now she had discovered that when he'd said her body was perfect what he really meant was that it was *perfect for having babies*! Not perfect for sin and seduction! He just had a burning desire for children, and for some reason she was the one chosen to help him fulfil his ambition. He saw her as a wife and a mother rather than as a voluptuous sex siren.

She felt totally and utterly deflated.

On impulse she abandoned her packing, stripped off her

shapeless dress and stood in front of the mirror in her under-wear. What did he see when he looked at her?

Full breasts. *Child-bearing hips*.

Brushing the tears from her cheeks, she turned sideways and stared at her outline. He'd chosen her as a wife capable of breeding a family, not as a life partner he could love, cherish and have fun with. *Share with*.

And yet why should his attitude surprise her. *Why?*

He was Sicilian and she'd always known that.

Wasn't that the whole reason she'd run in the first place?

How could she have forgotten?

Tears still soaking her cheeks, she slid back into her dress and sank onto the edge of the bed, forcing herself to face the painful truth.

He didn't love her and he'd never love her.

For him, their relationship was all about having babies. Creating a big, noisy Sicilian family full of big, fat sons groomed to carry on the macho tradition.

She blew her nose hard, and then looked up as the door crashed open and Rocco strode into the room. Strands of glossy dark hair fell over his bronzed forehead and his dark eyes glimmered with volcanic fury.

'Go away—' She scrunched the tissue into a ball and turned her head to hide her blotched cheeks. She didn't want to give him the satisfaction of seeing her crying. 'I don't have anything to say to you.'

'And yet you came to my offices so that we could talk, did you not?' He pushed the door shut, and suddenly the enormous bedroom seemed impossibly claustrophobic.

'Just leave me alone,' she muttered, sliding back onto the bed and drawing her knees up against her chest. 'I don't like you. I wish I'd never come back to Sicily.'

'I would have tracked you down.' She felt the bed move as he sat down next to her. 'If this marriage of ours is ever going to work, you have to stop running away.'

'I'll stop running away when you stop giving me cause!' She lifted her head and glared at him, suddenly indifferent to her blotched cheeks. 'Do you want to know why I left the night of our wedding? Because I suddenly discovered that you are *exactly* like my father.'

The anger in his eyes was replaced by wary incomprehension. 'Francesca—'

'They were all talking about you—did you know that?' She blew her nose again, and then wiped her eyes on the heel of her hand. 'I was standing there, in my stupid frothy wedding dress, thinking I was the luckiest girl in the world, and I heard them talking. A whole group of them.'

'Who?'

'You should know! You've obviously slept with all of them,' she muttered, covering her face with her hands as she recalled the conversation. 'They were talking about *me*. They said that you'd married me because I was meek and compliant and that was what you wanted in a wife. I think the exact quote was, "No modern woman in her right mind would marry a man like Rocco, rich and gorgeous though he is."'

'They were clearly jealous because they hadn't been offered the opportunity,' Rocco said smoothly, prising her hands away from her face with determination. 'Look at me, Chessie!'

'They said that Lorna had nothing to worry about because you'd carry on seeing her after we were married.'

'They were *trying* to hurt you,' Rocco breathed, but Chessie shook her head.

'They didn't know I was there.' She abandoned the

crumpled tissue and yanked another from the box. 'But I decided that I'd find you and talk to you about it.'

Rocco tensed and released her hands. 'So why didn't you?'

'I did! And you were on the terrace, laughing with Lorna and kissing her.'

'I've known her a long time.'

Chessie covered her ears. 'I don't want to know. I really, really don't want to know. I just want you to agree to a divorce.'

'You're being ridiculous. Lorna and I were not together in the way you mean. And those women were just being spiteful.'

She dropped her hands and looked at him. 'I watched the same thing happen to my mother,' she whispered, and his mouth tightened.

'*What* did you watch happening to your mother?'

'I watched my father slowly break her heart and then her spirit. My mother was his wife, and yet she shared nothing with him. There were no romantic gestures, no caring. Nothing.'

'It was your mother who encouraged you to run away that night, wasn't it?'

Chessie nodded. What was the point in lying? 'She wanted me to do what she'd never had the courage to do. Have a life of my own. She gave me the money I needed to make a fresh start, away from my father.'

'And Carlo? I know that you didn't sleep with him, but were you close?'

Chessie hesitated. 'He was my father's gardener,' she admitted finally. 'I barely knew him, but he was leaving to take a job in Rome and my mother had enough money saved up to persuade him to give me a lift as far as the ferry.'

'He dropped you at the ferry? That's all?'

'That's right. After we docked he drove off. I didn't see him again.'

There was a long silence while Rocco digested this piece of information. Then he rose to his feet in a fluid movement, his broad shoulders tense as he paced the length of the room. 'I thought you had a relationship with him.'

'No. Before that night we had exchanged fewer than ten words.' Why was he still dwelling on her relationship with Carlo? Chessie gave a humourless laugh as she studied the tension in his frame. Because he saw her as a possession and all he cared about was keeping his possessions exclusive. How could she have believed that Rocco genuinely liked her? He might be a different generation from her father, but in terms of attitude, no progress had been made. 'Your problem is that you're living in the wrong era. You'd be entirely comfortable in the Stone Age, living in a cave with a willing woman waiting by the fire to greet you after you've cleaned your weapon after a day's hunting.'

He turned, one dark brow raised in question. 'And what's wrong with that?'

She glanced at him in disbelief. 'Haven't you ever heard of evolution? Man has moved on, Rocco.'

'Which is why you're now living in a villa and not a cave.' He waved a hand as if to prove his point. 'You have a beautiful home.'

He just didn't get it. Tears threatened again, and she covered her face with her hands. 'Just get out, Rocco.' She felt the bed move slightly as he sat down next to her once again.

'Whatever you may think about me, I do *not* like seeing you this upset,' he breathed, pulling her hands away from her face and forcing her to look at him. 'I can see we've had a major misunderstanding here, but we can fix it.'

'We have different personalities,' Chessie said thickly,

reaching for yet another tissue and blowing her nose hard. 'I don't see how we can ever fix that.'

'Different personalities is good,' Rocco assured her, a faint smile touching his hard mouth as he scrubbed away her tears with the pad of his thumb. 'If we were the same then we'd clash all the time.'

Chessie sniffed. 'We *are* clashing.'

'No, we're not. We've just had a slight difference of opinion.' He dismissed it with a careless wave of his hand. 'Whatever you may think, I want our marriage to work.'

'Our marriage will never work.'

'It will work.' His rough, sexy voice made her nerve-endings tingle, but she rejected the sensation.

'How?' Her tone weary, she shredded the tissue clutched in her hands. 'I just can't begin to understand you, and it's perfectly clear that you can't begin to understand me either. And, given that we only ever meet to procreate, that isn't ever going to change.

'Children should be *part* of a relationship, not the whole reason for it. Our marriage isn't what I expected. There's no romance! No sharing!'

He looked at her stack of books on the table next to the bed, scanning the titles. 'Perhaps you should remember that the success of romantic fiction usually lies in its ability to transport the reader into a fantasy world.'

'A fantasy world? Why does a good relationship have to be a fantasy?'

'I'm just saying that you shouldn't be taken in by fiction. A relationship based on respect and understanding is far more successful than one based on physical lust. I've had those, and they've never lasted long,' he assured her, clearly oblivious to the depressing effect his words had on her.

She didn't know which was more upsetting—his tactless reminder of his numerous previous relationships, or the fact that he didn't see her as a candidate for physical lust. She wanted him to desire her! 'We have completely different aspirations and expectations,' she said flatly, and he shrugged dismissively, as if her observation posed no great problem.

'Then we will work to understand each other. You're obviously saying that you need more traditional romantic gestures, and I'm sure I can oblige—so you can unpack your bag.' He checked his watch and rose to his feet in a fluid athletic movement. 'And now I have to go back to work. I'm expecting a call from Tokyo.'

'I thought we were talking—'

'We've talked, and I've got the message. You don't want to have children immediately. Despite what you think of me, I can understand that. You're still very young. So we'll wait. And I'll be more romantic. Get some sleep. You must be very tired.'

After all that baby-making, Chessie thought to herself, but bit her lip to stop herself saying the words aloud.

It was obvious to her now that he had very fixed ideas about her role as a wife and mother, and they didn't coincide with her own. But how could she even begin to explain that she wanted him to find her sexy when that clearly wasn't what he looked for in a wife?

She stared at the bag she'd packed.

At least he'd bothered to come and talk to her. That was a start, wasn't it?

She sank back against the pillows, exhausted from the all the emotions, and she was still lying there when the first bunch of flowers arrived, exotic and confident.

Rocco's housekeeper Maria brought them into the

bedroom suite, with a beaming smile and a warm look of approval in her brown eyes.

'Beautiful, aren't they?'

Chessie stared. They *were* beautiful. And ordering them must have been the first thing Rocco had done on his return to the office. Despite her reservations about their relationship, she was touched.

'Was there a card?' Had Rocco included a few affectionate words? Her heart gave a little skip of anticipation, but Maria shook her head.

'No card.' The housekeeper arranged them in a vase and placed them in the centre of a table. 'They look beautiful there.'

'Yes. You're sure there was no card? No message?' *Nothing personal?*

'Flowers say a great deal all by themselves,' Maria said dreamily, and Chessie pulled herself together with an effort, trying not to be disappointed.

'You're right, of course.'

The second bouquet arrived half an hour later, and from then on one arrived every hour, on the hour, until dusk fell. By the time she'd eaten her lonely supper on the balcony, every surface in the room was crowded with scented blooms.

'Good job I don't suffer from hay fever,' Chessie murmured as she cleaned her teeth in the bathroom and then slid into bed.

But he was clearly making an effort, and she appreciated the gesture. And if a tiny part of her would have preferred just one bunch of flowers and a thoughtful note, another part reminded her that Rocco wasn't great with words and at least the flowers were a start. At least he was trying.

And she'd show him that she could try too. She'd unpacked her bag, and tonight she'd thank him. Properly. And this time their lovemaking would have absolutely nothing to do with making babies.

She lay in bed, hardly able to breathe as she waited for him to stroll through the door.

Tonight, she thought to herself, *everything is going to be different.*

It was going to be special.

She rolled over in the bed, her newly awakened body humming with delicious anticipation.

CHAPTER SIX

THE phone woke her from a fitful doze.

'How were the flowers?' It was Rocco, his voice smooth and supremely confident.

One glance at the bed was enough to confirm that she'd spent the night alone. *He hadn't come to bed.*

'Where were you last night?' Struggling to throw off the cloud of sleep, she rubbed her eyes. 'You didn't come to bed.'

'I left you to sleep.'

She felt the dull ache of disappointment. 'I—I was expecting you. I thought we could—' She broke off, suddenly realising that she had absolutely no idea how to tell her husband that she'd wanted sex. She'd never flirted with a man before, let alone seduced anyone. How was she supposed to tell him that she needed to know he found her attractive? 'You usually spend the night with me,' she muttered lamely.

'You don't want children yet, and I'm trying to respect that,' Rocco replied immediately. 'I'm happy for you to spend some time getting used to married life. Of course when you think you're ready just say the word and we'll be burning up the sheets in an instant.'

Discovering that there was nothing like anger and frustration for providing an effective wake-up call, Chessie sat up in bed. 'So what you're saying is that you don't want to spend the night with me unless we're making a baby.'

'Francesca—'

'You're supposed to have a PhD in women, but you don't know *anything*.' Her passionate declaration was greeted by a tense silence.

'You are making no sense at all,' he growled. 'You said you weren't ready for children so I'm staying away from you. I'm being thoughtful.'

Which basically meant that he didn't find her attractive. If a man found a woman irresistible, surely by definition he wouldn't be *able* to stay away?

Chessie flopped back against the pillows, too demoralised to argue.

'The flowers are lovely,' she said finally, deciding that she ought at least to acknowledge the gesture. 'There seems to be every type of bloom ever grown.'

'Good. My assistant wanted to know your favourite, and I didn't have a clue so she decided it was safest to order everything.'

Chessie closed her eyes, wondering if he even realised what he'd just said. His assistant. So the gesture hadn't even been his own. She could almost see him ticking the boxes. Romantic gesture means flowers. 'They're great.'

'She suggested that I ask you your favourite for future reference.'

'Deadly Nightshade,' Chessie muttered under her breath. 'So that I can crush it into your drink and poison you.'

'You're mumbling. I can't hear you properly.'

'Roses,' Chessie said flatly. *Maybe she could stab him with the thorns.*

'I'll tell her. At least now you can see that I'm capable of romance.' His tone was businesslike. 'There are some matters which require my personal attention over the next few days, so I left the villa yesterday. I'll see you when I'm back.'

'Right.' What difference would it make, Chessie thought numbly, when she didn't see him anyway?

'I think you should go shopping. Just speak to Max, my head of security. He'll arrange it. Feel free to spend my money.'

On what? she wanted to ask, but bit her lip 'Thanks.'

'When I come back, we'll talk again.'

'Right.' Chessie wanted to scream at him that she didn't *want* to spend his money or talk. What was the point of talking when they were on a completely different wavelength? She wanted *passion*! She wanted hot, steamy sex with a man who desired her so completely that he couldn't remember his own name, let alone the fact that he had business commitments.

But Rocco didn't associate her with hot, steamy sex. He didn't see her as a lover, and the word romance didn't enter his vocabulary. He saw her as a wife.

How was she ever going to change that? 'Where are you, anyway?'

'I'm in Florence. I hope to be home in another two days.'

Florence? Chessie felt the envy bubble up and swamp her as she thought of all the books she'd read and the art she'd studied in so much detail. 'You lucky thing. I'd love to see Florence,' she said in a husky voice. 'How long are you going to be there?'

'Not long enough for sightseeing. Another time, maybe. I'll bring you here and we can go shopping.'

Why would anyone want to visit Florence and waste time shopping? Chessie wondered. All she wanted to do was enjoy the art and architecture.

Reminding herself that he did have a job to do, and

couldn't be expected to act as tour guide, she didn't voice her disappointment. 'You poor thing, having to work so hard.'

At least he was making an effort, she told herself as she replaced the receiver and flopped back against the pillows. And he was obviously thinking of her. When he arrived home she was going to find some way of persuading him that fun in the bedroom didn't have to be restricted to making babies.

Suddenly hungry, Chessie sprang out of bed, showered, dressed and wandered through the cool, airy villa to the large, spacious kitchen.

The room was empty, but a half-drunk cup of coffee was on the table, and a television was on in the corner of the room with the sound muted.

Chessie reached for the coffee pot, and then froze as pictures of Rocco appeared on the screen, apparently leaving a Florence nightclub, his arm around a sexy, sleek blonde in a skirt so short it barely covered her bottom.

It wasn't Lorna. Which meant that he was with someone new.

This was the news. Which meant that the picture had been taken the previous evening. When he'd supposedly been in Florence on business.

Business?

She stared at the blonde.

When he'd told her that he was working she'd believed him, but instead—

She sank onto the nearest chair, struggling to breathe. She'd done it again. Believed in him. Believed that in his own way he cared about their marriage. *Given him the benefit of the doubt.* But his assistant had sent the flowers and he wasn't working hard at all. He was partying with another woman— an extremely sexy woman—while she, his wife, sat at home waiting for him to return.

How could she have been so stupid?

At what point had she forgotten that Rocco was Sicilian? When he'd said that she could postpone having children, she'd assumed that he intended to use the time to improve their relationship. Instead of which it was obvious that she was just supposed to do her own thing while he went out and enjoyed himself. And when she was ready to have children, he'd come back to her and perform the necessary biological function.

She ground her teeth with frustration.

When had he ever taken *her* out? When had he ever shown any inclination to spend time with *her*? It was obvious that if he wanted fun and enjoyment then he'd choose another woman.

He was her father all over again.

Her father had married her mother and then proceeded to spend their entire married life sleeping with other women. Marriage for him had been the respectable, socially responsible way of bringing children into the world while enjoying yourself on the side, and clearly Rocco was the same.

Wife. Mistress. Two separate roles with entirely different briefs. Her job was to stay at home, with her good, childbearing hips, and breed and feed their children. The mistress's job was to have endless sex for pure pleasure and indulge in other fun pursuits.

Unless she could persuade him to change his attitude.

Chessie glanced down at herself, trying to see herself through his eyes. Shapeless skirt. Shapeless top. Perhaps it wasn't entirely his fault that he didn't see her as a sex siren. If she wanted Rocco to see her as sexy then surely the first thing she had to do was actually try and *look* sexy? If she wanted him to look at her differently then she had to start looking like a woman he might choose to date—and she certainly didn't at the moment.

Casting her mind back to the girl on the television, she mentally evaluated the outfit she'd been wearing. Short skirt, high heels, revealing neckline. Hair loose and sexily dishevelled. At least she didn't need to be ashamed of her height. It didn't matter how high her heels were, the one thing she could guarantee was that Rocco, with his impressive build, would be taller than her.

Still in a daze, she stood up and walked back through the villa.

'Is everything all right, *signora*?' Max, the security chief at the villa, looked at her with consternation. 'You look very pale. Can I get you a glass of water?'

On the verge of confessing that she didn't need a glass of water, she needed a new wardrobe, Chessie stopped herself and thought quickly. 'Rocco said you'd be able to arrange a shopping trip before my journey to Florence?'

'You're joining him in Florence, *signora*?'

'In time for a night on the town,' Chessie said with a smile. 'I'm supposed to ask you to sort everything out. I'm meeting him at his favourite nightclub tonight. It's called—it's called…' She pretended to flounder and Max quickly supplied a name.

'That's right.' Her smile widened. 'That's the one. Perfect.'

'Do you want me to arrange for you to fly to Florence, *signora*?'

'I certainly do, Max.' She beamed gratefully. 'But do you know what? We need to go via some *seriously* expensive shops. Would you believe that I don't have a single suitable thing to wear?'

'I'll make the necessary arrangements.'

'And, Max—?' Chessie licked dry lips, trying to look casual. 'Do you happen to know a good hairdresser?'

'Of course.' Unconcerned by the request, he gave a nod. 'I'll arrange that too.'

Trying not to mind that Max had obviously been required to make similar arrangements for other women, Chessie smiled. 'Thank you.' She bit back a sudden impulse to grill him on her husband's favourite type of woman.

'I'll arrange for someone to pack your things, *signora*.'

Chessie opened her mouth to say yes, and then closed it again. 'Don't worry about packing, Max, because I'm going to have *new* things,' she said sweetly, suddenly remembering Rocco's claim that she had access to his immense wealth.

He'd probably made that statement safe in the knowledge that her taste didn't run to the glamorous.

Which meant that he was in for a shock.

Not only was she going to show him that her taste was perfectly capable of running to the *extremely* glamorous, but she was also going to teach him that it was possible for one woman to play a great number of parts—including wife *and* mistress.

'You're sure this skirt isn't too short?' Four hours later, Chessie scrutinised her reflection from every angle, feeling horribly naked and self-conscious. It was like wearing underwear and very little else. Did women really go out looking like this? She had an uncomfortable vision of herself being arrested for indecency and Rocco refusing to bail her out because he didn't recognise her as his wife.

'You have legs that most women would kill for, *signora*. Why cover them up?' The stylist fussed around her, narrowing her eyes as she assessed the finished result. 'There aren't many women who can wear that particular skirt, but you're one of them. And that halter top is perfect on you. It actually provides all the support you need while looking incredibly glamorous.'

Glamorous? *Did* she look glamorous? Unconvinced,

Chessie tilted her head left and right, examining the sparkly silver material that was cut to expose a tempting amount of cleavage. 'My father would have fainted on the spot if he'd seen me in this outfit—'

'Everyone's father would faint at this outfit,' the stylist drawled, a wicked smile in her eyes as she slipped several bangles onto Chessie's slender wrist. 'It isn't designed for fathers. It's designed for lovers, with sex and seduction in mind.'

Sex and seduction.

Wasn't that exactly what she wanted?

Certainly it was exactly the sort of outfit that one of Rocco's skinny girlfriends might wear. Mindful of that fact, she asked the question that was preying on her mind.

'Does it make me look fat?'

'Fat?' The stylist looked genuinely startled by the question, and then gave a slow smile. 'Well, you've got a body, if that's what you mean, but fat? No. You curve in all the places that really matter to men. Be prepared to be besieged when you walk into that nightclub.'

Besieged? Chessie frowned slightly. She didn't want to be besieged. She just wanted Rocco to notice her.

'Now I just need to have my hair cut.'

'Not cut,' the stylist urged hastily. 'Just trimmed. The length is fantastic. You just need some layers and texture to soften the effect.'

Never having been near a hairdresser, Chessie didn't have the first clue what the other girl was talking about, and in the end she just put herself in the hands of the hairdresser and crossed her fingers. He, in turn, ordered a deep conditioning treatment and then proceeded to cut soft layers into her hair until it fell around her face and over her shoulders in a seductive curtain.

Amazed by how different she looked, and unable to stop peeping at herself in the mirror, Chessie sat passive while someone did her nails and make up.

If this was how long Rocco's lovers took to get ready every time they went out, she thought to herself, then it was little wonder that they didn't have time for more serious commitments or a job. Being beautiful was definitely a full-time occupation.

Finally she left the salon and slid into the limousine that was waiting for her. But as they drove through the outskirts of Florence, Chessie felt her new-found confidence drain away.

It was all very well, dressing in a seductive way, but she had to learn to behave in a similar fashion and she wasn't sure she was up to it. She kept tugging at the hem of her skirt, and checking her cleavage to check she wasn't displaying too much.

Trying to boost her flagging confidence, she reminded herself that she looked *good*. In fact she couldn't wait to see Rocco's face when he realised that his wife was capable of being a sex siren. Comparing the way she looked now with her usual appearance, she came to the uncomfortable conclusion that it probably was her fault that up until now he'd only ever thought about her in the role of mother. After all, she'd hardly given him cause to think differently, had she?

But things were about to change.

When he saw her he was going to realise that his wife was also a living, breathing, sexy woman.

Their whole relationship was about to change for the better.

All the same, when the car finally drew up outside the nightclub that Max had assured her Rocco would be frequenting that night, she felt almost sick with nerves.

Hoping that she wouldn't fall and break something vital, trying to walk in her ridiculously high heels, Chessie reached for her bag. 'Don't wait for me,' she told the driver as she slid gingerly from the car, 'because I'm going to be a while.'

She teetered past the man policing the door and picked her way carefully down the marble stairs that wound into the darkness of the nightclub. Lights swirled, music pounded, and for a moment she just stopped and stared, amazed by the frenetic atmosphere. As her eyes adjusted to the lack of light, she noticed that the club was quite large, with a central dance floor surrounded by a seating area, and an ultra-modern-looking bar made out of glass and chrome.

Fascinated by the vibrant energy of the people on the dance floor, Chessie watched with admiration and a touch of envy as a woman lifted her arms high and swayed her hips in blatant invitation to her partner. Wondering what it would be like to be that uninhibited, Chessie watched a few others, seeking clues as to how they managed to dance in the heels.

'Fancy joining them? I can't believe someone as beautiful as you can possibly find herself without a partner, but I'm more than willing to oblige,' came a slurred male voice from beside her, and she turned to find herself uncomfortably close to a tall, handsome Italian man.

'Oh, no—I'm not on my own.' Realising that his eyes were fastened on the dip in her cleavage, she struggled against the impulse to cover herself. 'I'm with someone.'

'And he left you alone?' He moved closer. 'Is he a fool?'

'I—He—' Chessie's eyes slid back to the crowd and she felt a rush of relief as she saw Rocco saunter onto the dance floor. Relief turned to sick disappointment when she saw that his hand was locked around the wrist of a very beautiful blonde. Was it the same blonde he'd been with the previous night? Chessie narrowed her eyes. Same blonde. Different outfit.

'I see him.' A spark of anger igniting her flagging courage, she clutched her bag tightly and walked onto the dance floor, weaving her way through swaying couples until she reached Rocco.

He hadn't seen her approach, and was smiling down into the teasing blue eyes of his blonde companion, the warmth of his gaze unmistakable.

Ignoring an impulse that told her to just run and hide, Chessie sucked in a deep breath, reached up and tapped him on the shoulder. 'Excuse me.' Her voice barely carried over the throbbing music, but he turned instantly and stilled, his blank, discouraging look giving way to recognition.

'Francesca?' Even above the music she could hear the shock and disbelief in his tone. *'What* are you doing here?'

Prepared for a look of stunned admiration, and seeing something entirely different in his eyes, Chessie felt her courage falter. 'I was missing you.'

For a moment he didn't reply, and she watched as he inhaled deeply and took a good look at her. His eyes rested on the silky conditioned length of her beautifully cut hair before travelling slowly down over her bare shoulders, her exposed cleavage and the long length of sheer-stockinged leg. Shock turned to incredulity, and then to glowering disapproval.

Only when his eyes reached her vertiginous heels did he finally recover his powers of speech.

'What have you done to yourself?'

It wasn't the question she'd been expecting. 'Dressed up?' She could barely hear him over the pounding music, but it was obvious from the thunderous expression in his eyes that he was less than pleased with her appearance. Suddenly her confidence died a dramatic death.

Which bit of her outfit wasn't right?

A surreptitious glance behind him was enough to confirm that his companion for the evening was dressed in a similar manner, although admittedly on her the clothes looked different. But surely that was because the girl was extremely flat-chested and slim-hipped?

Chessie bit her lip. She could change her outfit, but she couldn't change her curves.

'Rocco—' Clearly resenting the competition for his attention, the girl curled perfectly manicured red nails over his arm. But he shrugged her away impatiently, his eyes still on Chessie.

'This place isn't appropriate for you.'

'Why not?' Her gaze challenged him, the spark in her eyes concealing the distinct quake in her stomach.

He was about to answer, and then something over her left shoulder made his face darken alarmingly. Wondering what could possibly have triggered such a volcanic response, Chessie turned to find the man she'd met at the entrance hovering behind her. He ignored Rocco and gave her a suggestive smile.

'How about that dance? Looks like your partner already has his hands full, so you might as well make do with me.'

She opened her mouth to refuse, and then closed it again. She was standing in the middle of a dance floor making a complete fool of herself over a man who didn't care about her. At least dancing with someone else would help to restore her dignity. 'Why not?'

The man reached out to take her hand, but Chessie felt strong fingers bite into her shoulder and she was jerked backwards into Rocco's hard, muscular body.

'She isn't dancing,' he said icily. 'And she's with me.'

The blonde girl shot Chessie a malevolent look and stalked off the dance floor, but Rocco seemed oblivious to the fall-out of his actions. Instead he released Chessie and shrugged out of his jacket, his eyes fixed on her beautifully made-up face. 'Put this on. Now.'

'I most certainly will not. It doesn't match what I'm wearing and it will cover up my new clothes.' Chessie moved slightly, so that the jacket slid into a pool on the floor.

'That's the general idea,' Rocco said through gritted teeth as he stooped to retrieve it. 'I *want* to cover you up. You're making an exhibition of yourself.'

'What about the girl you were with? Wasn't *she* making an exhibition of herself?'

'She isn't my wife.'

'Thanks for reminding me,' Chessie said flatly, and Rocco's eyes smouldered with building anger.

'I *won't* discuss this with you here. We're leaving.'

'Leaving?' Chessie stepped away from him. 'I'm not leaving. I've only just arrived, and you haven't even danced with me yet!'

'I'm not dancing with you when you're dressed like that. You're attracting enough attention without moving around.'

'What do you mean "dressed like that"? This is the way you like your women to look, Rocco. I look *exactly* like your girlfriend—except that I'm bigger in certain places over which I have absolutely no control.' With the help of the ridiculously high heels she could almost look him in the eye. 'I don't understand what's wrong.'

A muscle flickered in his lean, bronzed jaw and his dark eyes glittered dangerously. 'I don't like the way you look.'

Something died inside her. 'Well, I can't do much about that,' she mumbled, glancing towards the man who'd asked her to dance. '*He* didn't seem to find me repulsive.'

Rocco's dark jaw tensed and the expression in his eyes was menacing. 'Call me old-fashioned,' he growled, 'but I don't want my wife to be considered an object of lust by other men.'

'Well, you don't seem to want me, so I don't understand the problem.'

Muttering something that she didn't catch, he closed his hand round her wrist again and virtually dragged her from the dance floor to the stairs.

Unaccustomed to walking in high heels, she almost twisted her ankle, and grabbed at his arm to save herself. 'Slow down, will you? I can't walk this fast in these shoes,' she gasped.

He shot her a glance that was blisteringly unsympathetic. 'Then perhaps you should have worn something more suitable.'

'What could be more suitable for a nightclub than killer heels?'

'You should have worn something flat.'

'Why would I do that? I've spent my life wearing "something flat", Rocco,' she muttered, trying to regain her balance. 'For once I wanted to see life from a different perspective. I don't see why you care. Your height is one of your few redeeming features.' She stumbled again, and he let out an exasperated sigh and scooped her into his arms, striding through the door and outside onto the pavement without so much as a sideways glance at the doorman.

A flashbulb exploded in their faces, and Rocco cursed fluently in both English and Italian as he strode across to the limo that was waiting on the kerb. 'That picture will be all over the papers tomorrow. My wife being carried out of a nightclub.' He deposited her in the back seat and the door slammed shut behind them, shielding them from view. 'They won't know that you can't walk in heels. They'll assume you're drunk.'

'Why do you care? You've never cared what people think about you. Your reputation is confirmation of that.'

'Incriminating pictures never go away, and I don't want my

son having to see pictures of his mother being carried out of a nightclub.'

She collapsed back against the seat. 'So we're back to your son again? Don't you ever give up?'

'Obviously I was talking about the future,' he said coldly, and she turned her head to look at him.

'So what's your son going to think when he sees all the pictures of you with other women? Is he going to think *Way to go, Dad!* Or is he going to think *Stupid Mum, staying with that bastard?*'

Rocco inhaled sharply, and his gaze was icy and disapproving. 'Bad language doesn't suit you. It isn't in your nature.'

'How would you know what's in my nature? You've never taken the trouble to find out. You just have baby-making sex with me and then leave. My personality is obviously of as little interest to you as the rest of our relationship.'

There was a long, pulsing silence, and she was suddenly aware of the rapid escalation of tension in the car. The atmosphere cracked and snapped and Rocco stared at her, his breathing unsteady as his eyes dropped to her cleavage.

Then he dragged his eyes away and thrust his jacket towards her again. 'Put this on. And this time don't argue.'

'Why should I put it on? We're not in the nightclub any more.'

Like a storm cloud obliterating the light, his eyes darkened. 'I have no desire for my chauffeur and bodyguard to become intimately acquainted with your body.' His eyes slid back to her long, slender legs, and for a moment he seemed to have trouble speaking. Then he gritted his teeth and looked away. 'You don't look like a respectable married woman.' His voice was hoarse, and she frowned for a moment.

A respectable married woman?

'Well, obviously I didn't *want* to look like a respectable married woman when I dressed to go to the nightclub,' she said, struggling to keep her tone reasonable and measured. 'I would have looked completely out of place. I've never looked sexy before, and I wanted to look sexy.'

He ran a hand over his face, apparently having trouble concentrating on the conversation. 'Why would you need to look sexy?'

'What sort of a question is that? Because I want you to find me attractive! I even chose new underwear—look.'

On impulse, she lifted her skirt several inches and had the satisfaction of seeing something dark and dangerous flare in his eyes before he inhaled sharply. '*Dio*, what do you think you're doing?' His voice strangled, he leaned forward and hit a button, closing the screen between them and the driver.

'Showing you my new underwear.' *Trying to get some sort of reaction from him.*

His gaze lifted to hers, his eyes burning hot. 'Francesca—'

If the clothes didn't do it then maybe the underwear would, she thought, deciding to go for broke. With an unconsciously sensuous movement, she wriggled out of the stretchy short skirt, revealing black lacy pants and suspenders.

He stared at her in blatant shock, his powerful body unnaturally still.

'Francesca—you can't—' He broke off and swore softly, and then jabbed his fingers through his hair. 'You have to stop this. You have to stop this *now*.'

'Stop what?' Acting on an instinct that was entirely new to her, she pulled off her top.

Rocco's gaze transferred itself to the rise and fall of her full breasts, barely contained inside the filmy black bra. He murmured something hoarse in Italian, and then switched back to English. 'You can't—' His voice cracked and he cleared his throat. 'I don't think—' Struggling to compose a coherent sentence, he gave up on words and hauled her across his lap.

His mouth came down on hers with determined force, and excitement exploded inside her. She felt the rough slide of his hands in her hair, felt his fingers dig into her scalp as he held her head to allow himself full access to her mouth. The kiss went on and on, until her world was spinning and her body was throbbing with desperation. Until she'd forgotten where they were and who they were. They were biting, gasping, feasting on each other, and then she felt his hands drop from her head to cup her bottom—heard his hoarse groan of masculine appreciation as he encountered warm female flesh.

It was out of control and desperate, and his hands gripped and guided, positioning her to his satisfaction, and then she felt the insistent probe of skilled fingers as he sought out the most intimate part of her. His touch was so maddeningly good that she couldn't hold back a gasp of excitement. She writhed against his hands, their mouths still locked in a fierce kiss, his body pumped up and hard under hers as they drove each other frantic.

Chessie forgot they were in the car. Everything was focused on the physical demands of their bodies, and suddenly she felt a desperate need for satisfaction. Driven by a force that she didn't recognise, she slid her hands down his body and fumbled frantically with his zip, feeling the thickness of his arousal straining against the soft fabric of his trousers.

Sobbing his name against his lips, she finally managed to free him, and then wriggled her hips to bring herself closer.

Without breaking the kiss Rocco lifted her in a smooth, easy movement and positioned her above him. Then he steadied her writhing hips with his strong hands and ground into her with a fierce thrust that brought a cry to her lips and a harsh groan to his.

She moved by instinct, her hair falling forward, her tongue meeting the seduction of his, as their frantic, rhythmic movements drove them to the borders of sanity.

When they finally exploded it was at the same time, and she gasped his name as her body contracted round the rhythmic thrust of his.

And still he didn't release her, holding her hips with his hands and her mouth with his until the vicious pulse of his body finally ceased.

Finally she lifted her head, and they both dragged in much needed air.

'Rocco—' Her voice shaking with emotion, overwhelmed by what they'd both shared, Chessie lowered her mouth to his again, this time in a gentle kiss that acknowledged the depth of their intimacy. For a moment he didn't respond. His eyes were closed, his thick, dark lashes brushing his bronzed cheeks, the line of his jaw darkened by stubble.

Finally he controlled his breathing sufficiently to speak. 'I was rough.' His voice was low and very male. 'Did I hurt you?'

She felt her stomach shift. 'No.' She spoke the words softly. 'It was incredible.'

He closed his eyes briefly. '*Dio*, I can't believe we just did that.'

'What's wrong with what we just did?'

'We had sex in the back of my car.' As if suddenly acknowledging the implication of his own words, he lifted her away from him and deposited her on the seat. In a few swift movements he adjusted his clothing, and then glanced towards her with a dark expression in his eyes. 'Get dressed.'

'We're married, Rocco! What's wrong with—?'

'Get dressed!'

Why was he so angry? He hadn't been able to resist her, and surely that was a good thing? It meant that there was hope for their marriage. It meant he found her sexy—*that their marriage wasn't all about making babies.*

'You're incredibly prudish for a man with such a shocking reputation with women.' Confused, and still weak from the intensity of their lovemaking, Chessie wriggled back into her skirt and top and gave her hair a shake. 'How do I look?'

'Like someone's extremely hot date,' he growled, and she was about to smile and thank him for the compliment when she registered the simmering anger in his eyes. Clearly the comment hadn't been intended as a compliment.

'You just lost control,' she pointed out in a shaky voice, pushing her hair out of her eyes. 'So *don't* tell me that you don't like the way I look.'

He inhaled deeply. 'I don't like the way you look.'

All the pleasure and warmth was extinguished, and pain shattered her fragile ego. 'You hypocrite, Rocco. Remember the girl you were dancing with last night and this evening? How closely did you look at her? Because she was the inspiration for my wardrobe.'

He looked away. 'You didn't see her before this evening, so that can't possibly be true.'

'I saw the pair of you on the news last night. Short skirt, low neckline, high heels. I presumed that was what you liked in a woman, seeing as you were obviously having a good time with her.'

His handsome features set and tense, he turned to look at her. 'There were pictures on the news?'

'What? Did you forget that we have television in Sicily?' Her voice rose as her courage returned. 'Did you think that your little secret was safe as long as you stayed on the mainland? Judging from the way you were wrapped around her, you didn't seem to have any significant problems with the way *she* was dressed.'

'*She* isn't my wife.'

'Thank you for pointing out the obvious.' She couldn't keep the pain out of her voice as she slid her arms into the jacket he'd dropped into her lap. All her pleasure in the success of her new look had suddenly evaporated, and she slumped back in the seat, her body shivering.

He frowned. 'You're feeling cold?'

She sat for a moment without answering. Then she turned her head to look at him. 'No, Rocco. I'm not feeling cold. I'm feeling *totally* humiliated. Have you any idea how it feels to see your husband dancing with a sexy girl and not even be allowed to compete?'

'You don't need to compete. You're wearing my ring on your finger.' He dismissed her statement with an impatient lift of his hand.

'Well, do you want to know something?' The lump in her throat almost choked her. 'At this point in time I'd rather not be wearing your ring. If you gave me the choice I'd rather be your mistress than your wife. I don't want to be left alone on a remote island in the Mediterranean, no matter how beautiful it is. I want to get out there and *live*. It's becoming infinitely clear to me that if I was your mistress I'd have a much more exciting time than I ever will as your wife.'

'You're talking nonsense.'

'You think so? Think about it from my point of view. Your mistress gets to dance in nightclubs and dress however she likes.' She hugged the jacket around her. 'You take her out, and I dare say you actually spend waking hours with her.'

'I don't have a mistress,' he growled. 'The only woman I've slept with since our wedding is you. I do, however, have a wide circle of friends, most of whom I've known for a long time. And, yes, we "go out" if I happen to be in the right city at the right time. It's called having a social life.'

'Well, forgive me for not recognising a social life when I see one! The problem is that I've never actually had one. All I know is that they're fun!'

He watched her for a long moment. 'And you can also have fun,' he said finally, clearly seizing the opportunity to make peace. 'Is this about money? We've never had a direct conversation about it, but whatever you may think I have never curtailed your spending. As my wife, you are free to spend whatever you wish.'

'On what, precisely?' She virtually threw the question at him. 'You've trapped me on a remote island, Rocco. There isn't a shop in sight. And even if I did manage to buy something, where would I wear it? Sitting on your terrace by myself? You never take me anywhere. This isn't about money, Rocco, it's about living my life the way I want to live it. I don't want to be a hermit. You won't let me leave, you won't give me a divorce, but I have to have *some* say in the way I spend my time! Is that really so unreasonable?'

'You're trying to tell me that you want to live your life in nightclubs? That's where you would prefer to spend your time?' He looked at her as though he'd never seen her before, and she ground her teeth with frustration.

'Maybe. I don't know! I've never been to one before tonight. What I'm saying is that I want to *find out*. I want to do things that I've never been allowed to do before. Things that other people take for granted.' She sank back against her seat, too choked to say any more. It was pointless trying to make him understand. He was *exactly* like her father. He believed that a wife's place was in the home, bringing up children. 'Marriage to you is like being sent to prison. You've locked me up and thrown away the key.'

He scanned her taut profile with mounting exasperation. 'Suddenly I'm a gaoler because I refuse to take my wife to a nightclub?'

'I'm just telling you how it feels.' By a supreme effort she managed to get the words past the lump in her throat. She was so upset that she didn't even notice that the car had stopped until the door opened and he nudged her gently.

'We've arrived.'

Too miserable even to bother looking at her surroundings, Chessie followed him into a building and up some stairs into a palatial bedroom suite.

She plopped down on the edge of the bed, oblivious to the beauty of the room. 'I suppose you're going back to that other woman now?'

With an exasperated glance in her direction, Rocco pushed the door shut with the flat of his hand. 'Stop talking rubbish.'

'Why is it rubbish?' Her teeth were chattering. 'Given that you're a highly sexed guy, obviously you're going to be getting it somewhere.'

He let out a stream of Italian. 'Since you returned to Sicily, the only woman I have had sex with is you.'

She wanted so badly to believe him. 'You're saying you've never slept with her?' Her voice was small and hurt, and he paced over to the window and stood with his back to her.

'No, I'm not saying that.' He ran a hand over the back of his neck and then turned to face her, his mouth set in a grim line. 'But it was a long time ago. Before I ever met you.'

'So you *have* slept with her?'

He hesitated, and then muttered something inaudible under his breath. 'I won't lie to you. She's an old friend, yes, but the sort of relationship you're describing is very much in the past.' His eyes glittered with exasperation. '*Why* are we even having this conversation? I have not been unfaithful to you.'

'But you find her attractive?'

'What sort of a question is that?'

'A perfectly natural one, given that I'm your wife and you don't seem to find *me* attractive.'

He exhaled sharply and jabbed his fingers through his hair. 'This is not the sort of conversation I expect to have with my wife.'

'Why not, Rocco? Because I was a virgin until just over two weeks ago? Believe me, I'm learning fast. You took her to a nightclub. What would have happened when the evening ended? Would you have dropped her home?'

'No, someone else would have dropped her home, because she doesn't live in this direction. I really don't understand your obsession with her. My relationship with her is in the past, and most people have a past, Chessie.'

'I don't have a past, and at this rate I'm not going to have a decent future either.' She leaned forward and eased the shoes from her aching feet.

'This conversation is nothing short of ridiculous.' He shook his head as if to clear it, and then strode to the other side of the bedroom, opened a cabinet and poured himself a large drink. 'You're my wife, Chessie. What more do you want?'

'Too much, obviously.' *She wanted him to find her irresistible.*

Knowing that she was making a complete fool of herself, Chessie gave a murmur of self disgust and sprinted through a door that she hoped led to a bathroom.

When she finally emerged, her tear-stained cheeks splashed with copious amounts of chilled water, the room was empty.

Rocco sat on the roof terrace of the *palazzo*, staring into the darkness, a large drink in his hand as he tried to reduce his tension levels. Dwelling on his actions of a few hours earlier, he delved deep for some sort of plausible explanation for his uncharacteristic behaviour.

He'd taken her in a wild heat of lust, without thought or care for their surroundings.

What the hell had he been thinking of?

The answer was sex, he acknowledged grimly as he lifted the glass to his lips and drank deeply. He'd been thinking of sex. Wild, basic, primitive sex, with a woman designed to drive a man to the very limits of self-control.

The only problem was that the woman in question was his wife. And he hadn't planned to feel that way about his wife.

He hadn't *wanted* to feel that way about his wife.

He of all people knew just how dangerous such intense passion could be. He should do. He'd spent his life avoiding it.

Where exactly had he gone wrong? He'd planned it all so carefully, and suddenly everything was getting out of hand— and the fact that she was now *was* crying downstairs did nothing for his already disturbed state of mind.

Feeling distinctly uncomfortable, he ran a hand over the back of his neck and forced himself to face the fact that he'd treated his wife to an almost aggressive display of masculine lust. In the circumstances, he could hardly blame Chessie for being so upset.

He'd treated her as a hot, sexy woman designed to drive a man wild, rather than as his wife and the prospective mother of his son.

It was her own fault, he told himself firmly. She'd dressed in an utterly provocative manner. He started to tell himself that any man would have responded in the same way, and then realised that he was deriving little comfort from that particular strand of logic. The mere *thought* of any other man seeing Chessie looking the way she had when she'd walked into the nightclub was enough to bring Rocco out in a sweat.

Never again, he vowed as he drained his drink. Never again was she going out in public dressed like that. In fact he didn't want her dressed like that in private, either.

He wanted to return to the way their relationship had been before she'd stripped down to black lacy underwear.

The memory triggered an instantaneous reaction of the most predictable variety, and he gritted his teeth, trying to picture her in unflattering, shapeless black.

She obviously wanted new clothes, and that was fine with him. With hindsight perhaps he *had* been a little remiss in leaving her at his villa without sufficient occupation to take her mind off his absence. Obviously she was bored. He'd take her shopping, but he was going to supervise the selection of her new wardrobe.

He'd make sure there was nothing remotely provocative about her clothing.

He'd make sure that every inch of her incredible body was covered.

Then he could go back to feeling the way he'd felt about her before she'd strolled into the nightclub.

The problem solved to his satisfaction, Rocco placed the empty glass on the table and rose to his feet. He didn't trust himself to share a bed with her in his current state of uncontrolled lust, so he decided on a brisk walk through the streets of Florence.

Tomorrow they'd go shopping.

And then he could erase the images currently in his head and replace them with something more suitable and infinitely more comfortable to live with.

CHAPTER SEVEN

CHESSIE woke early and found herself alone. It was obvious that Rocco hadn't spent even the smallest part of the night in bed with her. Disappointment twisted inside her even while she tried to reason with herself and face up to the facts.

What had she expected?

Despite their frenzied, erotic encounter in the car the previous night, it was obvious that he didn't really find her alluring. After all, hadn't she had to dress up and virtually strip to get his attention? Why would he bother sharing a bed with her?

She didn't expect him to love her, but the fact that he didn't really find her attractive either was the final straw. How could their marriage possibly survive under those circumstances? Their expectations were entirely different, and it was obvious that he wasn't going to change his opinion of her.

No doubt his next move would be to bundle her home to Sicily, out of the way.

But she wasn't going to go quietly.

Dressing in her usual unflattering trousers and top, she lifted her chin and went in search of Rocco's head of security.

She was in Florence, and she intended to make the most of it!

The fact that her marriage was a disaster didn't mean that

she couldn't enjoy her surroundings and make the best of the situation.

Beyond the marble entrance hall doors opened onto a courtyard, and Chessie wandered outside, drawn by the beauty of the arches and columns. It was an oasis of peace, protected from the buzz of Florence by the high walls. The centrepiece was an elaborate fountain, and the continuous gush of water had a cooling effect on the otherwise stifling heat. In the corners of the courtyard, placed with almost geometric precision, large terracotta pots nurtured elegantly shaped orange trees, heavily laden with ripe fruit. The creamy vanilla walls of the courtyard filtered the bright sunlight, creating volumes of welcome shade. It was tranquil and calming, and she suddenly decided that it would be a lovely place to spend a quiet morning. Perhaps she'd save the sightseeing for later.

Delving into her bag for the pad and pencil that she always carried, she started to draw, her hand making bold strokes over the page as she reproduced the architectural perfection of the courtyard. The minutes stretched into hours, and she might have spent all day lost in her drawing had the sound of firm footsteps not disturbed her.

'*What* are you doing out here?' Rocco's voice was exasperated and his expression was grim. 'Have you *any* idea how much trouble you've caused?'

'Trouble?' Shock at seeing him made her drop the pencil, and she stooped to retrieve it, her face flaming. 'How can I have possibly caused any trouble when I've been sitting in a courtyard?'

'Perhaps because no one *knew* you were sitting in a courtyard,' Rocco returned through gritted teeth. 'Everyone in the *palazzo* is currently searching for you.'

'Oh, dear.' Chessie gave a guilty smile. 'What a waste of time. Didn't they think to look outside?'

'Evidently not,' he muttered, inhaling sharply and removing his mobile phone from his pocket. He stabbed a button with his finger, spoke in rapid Italian, and then dropped the phone back in his pocket. 'You gave us a fright, *tesoro*.'

'Why?'

'Because we didn't know where you were.'

'You need to keep track of me, Rocco?' She closed the sketchpad. 'Not content with locking me away, you also need to know where I am every minute of the day? Perhaps you ought to just put an electronic tag on me and have done with it. Or tie me to a post on a long lead. You're being possessive again.'

He inhaled sharply. '*Not* possessive. Protective. And I cannot believe that even you could be that naïve about security. It isn't about locking you up or tracking your movements. It's about caring for your safety.'

Her heart skipped. 'What are you saying?'

'You want me to spell it out?' His eyes were hard. 'I'm a wealthy man. Naturally you're a target for those who would like to hurt me.'

It hadn't occurred to her. 'I was just enjoying the courtyard.'

'All morning?' He stared at her with blank incredulity. 'What exactly were you doing out here that would take all morning?'

'Nothing.' She tried to sneak the sketchpad behind her back, but Rocco strolled over to her, his hand extended.

'Show me.'

'There's nothing to see.'

'Then you won't mind showing me.'

He was an impossible man to argue with. Relinquishing the pad reluctantly, she turned her head, too embarrassed by her drawing to be able to view his reaction. 'This is a nice hotel. Surprisingly quiet. I haven't seen a single other guest all day.'

'There are no other guests, and that's because it isn't a hotel. It's my home.' His voice was thoughtful as he slowly lifted each page of the pad, studying the contents. 'How long have you been drawing, Chessie?'

Why lie? 'All my life. And before you say anything, I'm perfectly aware that I have absolutely no talent.' She watched as a tiny lizard scurried across the dry, dusty courtyard in search of shade. *That was what she wanted to do,* she thought. Hide. Only in her case she would be taking refuge from Rocco, not the sun. She braced herself for a derogatory comment, telling herself that his opinion didn't matter. 'I do it because I enjoy it. I find it relaxing. It's a way of escaping.'

He studied her for a long moment, his expression watchful, and then handed the pad back. 'I think you have exceptional talent,' he said in his usual decisive tone. 'Who made you think otherwise? Presumably it was the same person who made you think that you're fat and unattractive? Your father?'

'It doesn't matter.' Why was he being so nice? Was he just trying to make amends for the night before? 'Drawing is just something I've always done. It doesn't mean anything—'

'Is this the job you want? You want to draw?'

Startled, she looked at him, astonished by how astute he was. 'Why would you think that?'

'When I'm so insensitive about so many other things, you mean?' His tone was loaded with irony but there was humour in his eyes. 'I'm good at spotting talent in others. It's one of the things I do well. My company thrives on my ability to identify and nurture talent—especially talent that I don't possess myself. Answer my question. Your ambition is to draw professionally?'

'I don't know.' She gave a self-conscious shrug and studied the lizard again. 'I don't have the skills for that. No training. I just know I can't go a day without drawing. It's part of who I am.'

'You should have studied art at university.'

'I wasn't given the opportunity.' She stood up and glanced at him, and then wished she hadn't because her stomach lurched in instant response to his physical presence.

His hair was damp from the shower, his jaw freshly shaved and he smelt delicious. He was shockingly handsome, she thought despairingly. High cheekbones, bronzed skin, thick lashes—what woman could ever resist him? Memories of their passionate encounter the night before suddenly made her limbs weaken. Maybe she should just suggest they made a baby? she thought helplessly as she dragged her eyes away from his face. At least that way he'd take her back to bed.

'Did you just say that this place is your home? You actually live here?'

'When it suits me.' He was studying her face with brooding contemplation. 'I have several homes. I thought you knew that.'

'But I didn't know you had one in Florence.' She glanced around her. 'It's truly amazing. Like a palace.'

'It was originally a *palazzo*, built in the sixteenth century. Then there was a big family squabble about ownership and it was left to rot. It was a crumbling, neglected wreck when I bought it ten years ago. I've had a team working on its restoration ever since. It's coming along nicely.'

'Incredible,' Chessie breathed, her head tilted backwards as she looked at the height of the courtyard. 'Can I look round properly?'

'Later, when we're back from our trip.'

'Trip?' She dragged her eyes back to his. 'What trip? Don't you have to work today?'

'You've obviously been so involved in your drawing that you haven't noticed that it's already almost the afternoon. I worked most of the night and all through this morning. My wife is complaining that I've been neglecting her,' he said in a silky tone, 'so I intend to rectify that.'

'Oh. I assumed you'd send me back to Sicily.' She blushed slightly as she caught the sardonic gleam in his eye. 'So where are we going?'

'Shopping. If you want a new wardrobe then I'm prepared to buy you one. But I'm afraid I'm going to decide what's suitable and what isn't. No more appearing in public in your underwear.'

Chessie didn't know what to make of that comment. Was he trying to say that he'd liked the way she'd looked? No, obviously not, since he intended to buy her something entirely different.

'I don't really need clothes. I don't exactly go anywhere that requires dressing up.' Chessie scraped her fingers through her newly cut hair, which fell in a gratifyingly perfect sheet over one shoulder.

His eyes narrowed. 'They did a good job on your hair. It looks fantastic. And you *will* be going somewhere that requires new clothes, because I intend to take you for lunch.'

'Why?'

He frowned briefly, as if the thought hadn't previously occurred to him, then he shrugged. 'Why not?'

'I thought my role was to be locked up at home until I produce a brood of sons?'

'Don't push your luck, *tesoro*,' he warned, but there was amusement in his eyes as he stretched out a hand and took hers in a firm grasp. 'Today I'm taking you out. There are some questions I want to ask you. Questions that I probably should have asked a long time ago.'

There were some questions she wanted to ask him too—like why he was bothering—but he was already striding back into the *palazzo* and towards the door that led into the street.

Wondering if he knew the meaning of the word 'relax,' Chessie struggled to keep up, relieved that her shoes were more forgiving than the ones she'd worn the previous evening.

He took her to a small boutique in a quiet back street, away from the throng of tourists.

It was subdued and elegant, full of tall plants and creamy polished marble, and the sort of place that she would have been far too terrified to enter had he not pushed her inside in his usual decisive fashion.

Feeling horribly self-conscious, Chessie rifled through the rails. 'There are no prices.'

Rocco gave a faint smile. 'If you need to look at the prices then you probably can't afford to shop here. But fortunately you can, *angelo mio*. Choose something you like.'

'Don't you mean something *you* like?' she muttered, and his smile widened.

'Actually, yes, I suppose I do mean that.' He spoke without a trace of remorse. 'And what's wrong with that?'

She glanced at him with exasperation and gave a brief shake of her head. Still, at least he'd agreed that she needed clothes, which was a start, and he was taking her out. 'Where are you taking me?'

'I've already told you. Lunch.'

'Somewhere special?'

He gave a faint smile of amusement. 'Of course.'

'Then I'll need something summery but smart.'

Immediately her eye was caught by a summer dress. It was a vibrant shade of red with white spots. 'That's pretty. Is it decent enough for you?' Her sarcasm appeared lost on him.

'Try it on and I'll soon tell you.' He lifted it from the rail and handed it to the assistant who was hovering.

Five minutes later, Chessie was staring at herself in the floor-length mirror and trying not to drool. The dress was fabulous. Gorgeous. And, what was more, it fell below the knee—and the neckline would have satisfied a nun, so Rocco couldn't possibly object.

'Are you decent?' Rocco's deep, dark drawl came from outside the cubicle and she felt her pulse suddenly race. He couldn't possibly hate it, she assured herself as she unlocked the door and stood in front of him.

'Well?'

For a moment he didn't speak, and then his mouth tightened and his eyes hardened. 'You're not leaving this boutique dressed like that.'

Dressed like what?

Speechless and confused, she glanced at herself in the mirror, trying to see what she'd missed. Was the dress backless? Was it see-through? The answer was a definite no to both questions, and she turned back to him with a murmur of exasperation. 'I don't understand. What's wrong with it?'

'It shows every curve of your body. That's what's wrong with it.'

Anger and frustration started to bubble up inside her. 'Rocco.' With a huge effort, she kept her tone patient. 'Apart from the colour, this dress would not look out of place in a convent.'

His handsome face unsmiling, he turned to the assistant and gave her a brief on exactly what he wanted. Nothing low, nothing short, nothing revealing.

The woman hurried away, and eventually returned with armfuls of clothes. Chessie tried them on, her sense of frustration increasing as Rocco rejected them all as unsuitable, his dark eyes reflecting a slow-building anger.

As she paraded the eleventh item and he shook his head she felt her own temper begin to sizzle. 'Rocco, this is ridiculous. I have to wear *something*. These clothes are fabulous. Really, really stylish. What was the point of bringing me here if you're not going to let me buy anything? *You* suggested this shop. You were the one who said that it sold all the right things.'

He let out a driven sigh and stabbed his fingers through his hair. 'I thought it would be fine, but it isn't. It's all too revealing.'

'Revealing?' Chessie grabbed a pair of trousers that he'd rejected and virtually thrust them under his nose 'What about these? They can hardly be described as revealing!'

His shoulders tensed. 'They clung to every curve.'

'They don't cling. They skim. They're well cut and perfectly decent.'

'Every man you pass will be looking at your bottom,' he growled, and she opened her mouth to protest and then closed it again, her mind suddenly racing.

'Because I have good child-bearing hips, you mean?'

'No.' He gave a humourless laugh. 'Because you have a bottom straight out of a bad man's dreams, that's why.'

Her heart and stomach gave a little flip. 'So what you're actually saying is that you really *like* my bottom?'

The tension in his powerful frame increased. 'Whether or not I like your bottom isn't the issue.' There was no trace of amusement in his gaze. 'The issue is whether I want to see your attributes on display, and I don't.' He was becoming more and more uptight, and Chessie suddenly started to feel better.

'So the reason that you don't want to see my bottom is not because you find me repulsive but because you don't want other men to admire me?' She handed the trousers to the assistant, who was hovering. 'Because you're jealous? That's the best news I've had for a long time, Rocco.'

'I'm not jealous,' he breathed. 'And I don't know why you're giving those trousers to her, because you're not having them. And I fail to see how the fact that I'm about to strangle you with my bare hands can possibly be good news for either of us.'

She gave him a womanly smile and had the satisfaction of seeing his gaze darken. 'Don't worry, Rocco,' she said soothingly, also handing the assistant two dresses, a lacy top and two jackets. 'I think you're just starting to come to terms with the fact that a man *can* see his wife as something other than a baby producing machine. You find me sexy, don't you? You don't want to, but you do. Be honest.'

He inhaled sharply. 'Francesca—'

'Admit it, Rocco.' She lowered her voice so that only he could hear her. 'Last night in the car—'

'I *don't* want to talk about last night.'

'Well, I do—because it's really important. You wanted me. Badly. Not because you wanted to make babies, but because you wanted to have wild and abandoned sex. You kept holding back, and I thought it was because you didn't find me attractive. But I'm starting to think that you *do*. And you're not at all comfortable with that because I'm your wife, and you have this distorted idea that you're not supposed to feel that way about me.'

He froze, his jaw suddenly tense. 'I can't believe we're having this conversation. We're standing in a dress shop.'

'Boutique,' Chessie said sweetly, standing on tiptoe to kiss his cheek. Suddenly she felt impossibly light-headed and happy. 'Stop looking so uptight. I like the fact that you find me sexy. It's what I wanted. Now I just need you to ravish me the way you did in the car.'

His shoulders stiffened. 'I hurt you,' he said in a hoarse voice. 'You were crying in your room last night.'

'Because you walked away from me. You didn't hurt me, Rocco. I loved what we did.'

His jaw was clenched. 'We won't be doing it again. Not like that.'

'Yes, we will, Rocco.' Her voice was soft. 'And just to make sure of it you're going to take me to a lingerie shop next.'

'Lingerie?' He said the word as though it were stuck in his throat, and her smile widened.

'Yes, lingerie. Why not? The sexier the better.' She allowed her tongue to linger over the words and had the satisfaction of seeing his breathing quicken. 'The sort that bad men fantasise about, along with the body inside. The sort I was wearing last night when you completely forgot that I was your wife and that we were in the back of your car. The sort designed for seduction.'

His bronze cheeks lost some of their colour. 'And just who are you planning to seduce?'

'You, of course.' She breathed the words softly, so that they couldn't be overheard. 'So far you've done all the seducing, but that's about to change. We're married, Rocco. Seduction should be part of the job description. I'm not talking about making babies. I'm talking about making love.'

'Francesca—' He slid a finger inside the collar of his shirt and swore softly. 'Chessie—'

Loving the fact that he seemed lost for words for the first time in their relationship, she stood on tiptoe again and leaned closer, a smile touching her mouth as she whispered against his ear. 'Are you going to hand me your wallet, or would you like me to search for it?'

With a smouldering glance that promised retribution, Rocco produced his credit card and handed it to the enraptured assistant. 'Don't think you're wearing any of those clothes outside the *palazzo*,' he growled under his breath, but Chessie's smile simply brightened as she walked past him to pick up the small mountain of bags.

He found her sexy.

Rocco really, really found her sexy.

He might not want to find her sexy. He might want to think that having a wife was all about producing babies. But that didn't change the fact that he thought she looked good in the clothes. Too good.

All she had to do now was try and loosen him up a little. Persuade him that it was perfectly acceptable to desire his own wife.

'How far is this restaurant?'

'A short drive.' They'd swapped the limousine for a low, lethal-looking Maserati, and Rocco drove with the relaxed skill of a racing driver as he put the car through its paces on the road out of the city. The engine gave a throaty growl, and people turned their heads to look and admire. 'It's on a hill. The views are incredible.'

'A short drive? Good. In that case, close your eyes.' Opening one of the bags, she dipped inside and pulled out the spotty dress. Then she slid lower in her seat and pulled off her top.

The car swerved dangerously. 'What are you *doing*?'

'Changing?' She wriggled into the dress and then slid out of her trousers. 'I want to wear this dress to lunch. Shouldn't you keep your eyes on the road?'

A muscle worked in his jaw as he tightened his hands on the wheel. 'You can't undress in public.'

'Calm down. I've already done it. No one noticed.'

'*I* noticed,' he said and she smiled.

'Good. You were supposed to.' Loving the feel of the dress against her body, Chessie dipped into another bag, this time retrieving the shoes she'd purchased to go with the dress. Finally she gave her newly cut hair a shake and applied a touch of gloss to her mouth. 'You're not watching the road again, Rocco.'

'With you half-naked next to me, is that really surprising? I'm wondering what happened to the demure, innocent girl I married,' he muttered, and she slid across the seat towards him, smiling as the wind blew her hair across her face.

'I might have been innocent, but I was never demure. Just repressed. But I'm getting over that now,' she said happily, her gaze flirtatious as she slid her hand over his shoulder and looked up at him. 'I speak my mind with you.'

'I'd noticed.'

'And it's very exciting, knowing that I can try doing new things.'

The hard muscle of his shoulder tensed under her fingers. 'What new things, exactly?'

'I've no idea. I've never been free to do whatever I like before.'

'And you're not free to do whatever you like now,' he reminded her in flinty tones. 'Perhaps this is a good time to remind you that, whatever you plan on trying, I'm going to be standing right next to you.'

Chessie relaxed back against the seat and closed her eyes, enjoying the decadent feeling of the open topped car. 'That's fine by me. I love this car, by the way.'

'I don't understand you at all.' She caught the exasperation in his tone and her smile was sympathetic.

'I suspect you've never understood *any* woman before now—
but there's always a first time, and I've always been an optimist.'

She wanted him to understand her?

Not a cat in hell's chance, Rocco thought wryly as he
guided her onto the terrace of the restaurant. She was a mass
of contradictions.

She walked in front of him and he immediately forgot
what it was he was supposed to understand—because he
found himself utterly transfixed by the tempting curve of her
bottom. She walked with a graceful, swaying motion that
was unconsciously sexy and almost painfully alluring, and it
took only one glance for him to confirm that every male eye
in the restaurant was fixed on his wife.

Feeling his stress levels soar, Rocco ran a hand over the
back of his neck and wondered what had possessed him to
take her shopping.

He should have left her in drab black.

He'd *liked* her in drab black. It was safe, and it didn't give
him problems with his blood pressure.

The change in her was astonishing—and it wasn't just the
clothes. It was the way she carried herself, as if she'd suddenly
discovered the meaning of the word confidence.

Accustomed to the heat and humidity of an Italian summer,
Rocco suddenly wondered why the air seemed so stifling.

With the incident in the car still painfully fresh in his mind,
he dragged his gaze away from her tempting curves and tried
to concentrate on something suitably boring and safe.

When he'd married Chessie he'd been drawn to her sweet
nature and her timidity. Coming to terms with the fact that his

wife had transformed herself into a sex siren was requiring some significant adaptation on his part.

He was still recalling every detail of their steamy encounter in the car with an uncomfortable degree of clarity, and no matter how hard he concentrated, he was unable to look at her in the same way.

If he looked at her hair he just remembered it soft and tangled, falling over his face as they'd kissed and made love.

If he looked at her mouth he just remembered the desperate little moans she'd made as they'd kissed and made love.

If he looked at her body he just remembered the sensuous writhing of her hips as they'd kissed and made love.

Deciding that the only way to preserve his sanity was to concentrate on the menu and the view, Rocco struggled to find his customary control—and failed.

As they settled down at the best table in the restaurant she gave a gasp of delight, oblivious to the fact that she was the object of attention from several quarters of the room. 'I can see the whole of Florence from here. Oh, Rocco, it's beautiful.'

She was sweet, he thought to himself. And she never chose her words for effect, as every other woman he knew did. Chessie just said what she thought. She didn't hold anything back.

The thought of her not holding anything back drew his mind again to her passionate response in the car, and Rocco hastily ordered drinks, struggling to control his suddenly ravenous libido.

Suddenly aware that the man at the table nearest to them was staring in open-mouthed appreciation at Chessie's generous curves, he glared a warning at him and wondered whether he should summon his helicopter and fly her back to Sicily.

'What's the matter?' Her tone was concerned. 'You seem really tense.'

She hadn't even noticed, he thought moodily. She was so innocent that she didn't even know when men were looking at her. 'I'm just wondering whether we should leave and go somewhere else.'

'Leave?' She looked genuinely astonished, and then her face fell. 'Why? This is perfect. It's beautiful here. I love it.'

Reflecting on the fact that most women of his acquaintance would have considered it seriously uncool to show such enthusiasm, Rocco forced himself to relax and examine his own behaviour. Why did it bother him that another man was looking at Chessie? He'd always dated women that other men wanted, so it was hardly a new experience.

But he'd never before experienced such a powerful desire to lock one of them away, and before today he'd never in his life thought of himself as truly possessive.

She was his wife, he reasoned as he uncurled his fists and it was perfectly natural to be possessive about one's wife.

It didn't mean he was repeating mistakes of the past.

'All right, we'll stay. The fish in this restaurant is excellent,' he said shortly, and Chessie turned her head from her study of the view.

'Are you angry? You sound angry.'

'I'm not angry.' It was fine to be attracted to her. There was nothing wrong with that, and there was certainly no reason for him to feel uncomfortable about it.

Chessie was frowning at him as she sat back to allow the waiter to pour their drinks. 'Tense, then. Are you worried because you're missing a day of work?'

'I'm not tense.' He reached for his glass and drank deeply. A sideways glance told him that the man was still staring at

Chessie, and he was about to stand up and resort to violence when she leaned forward and touched his hand with her fingers, the gesture almost timid.

'I know this wasn't exactly what you planned to do with your day, but thank you,' she said softly, and he frowned.

'For what?'

'For bringing me here. For taking me out.' She gave a hesitant smile and glanced towards the view that stretched beneath them. 'It's spectacular. You couldn't have made a better choice for my first restaurant. I can't tell you how exciting it feels. Sitting up here with the view, and the sun on my face, and being with you—' She broke off and took a breath. 'It feels like being free. So, thank you.'

Her words shocked him so much he momentarily forgot about the man seated next to them. 'Your first restaurant? Are you seriously telling me that you've never been to a restaurant before? That isn't possible.'

Her smile faltered. 'When would I have been? You've never taken me.'

'But I've only known you for the past nine months. What about your life before that? And then you were on your own for six months.'

'I didn't go out then. I didn't dare.' She studied her plate and then lifted her eyes to his. 'I suppose there's no reason not to tell you now. I stayed with a family on a farm, near Naples. I met them on the ferry and they offered me a job and somewhere to live. Until the night I flew to Sicily I never left their farm.'

'Which is why my security team made such a dismal failure of finding you,' Rocco drawled, passing her some bread. 'And they were a nice family?'

'They were amazing. So different from mine.' Her tone

was envious. 'They had six children, and each one was encouraged to be independent and free-thinking. And the parents were interested in everything they had to say. They liked the fact that they were individuals. It took me a while to fit in.'

'Because you were shy?'

'Because I wasn't used to having my own thoughts, let alone expressing them.' Her voice was soft, and then she smiled. 'But they were great. They used to fire questions at me, and they were always asking my opinion. They made me feel as though I was strong enough to do anything. I learned to speak up.'

Rocco smiled. 'So I have them to thank for the transformation in my previously tongue-tied wife?'

'Probably. But this is the real me.'

He nodded. 'Your life at home was obviously extremely restricted. I had no idea how bad. Did you never go out with your father and mother? Family meals? Celebrations?'

The waiter placed their starters in front of them and Chessie picked up her fork. 'I don't think my father thought he had much to celebrate,' she said flatly, and Rocco watched her, wondering why he hadn't picked up on any of the clues before.

At what point had he developed such a pitiful lack of insight?

'I have several questions about your relationship with your father.'

'That's a topic designed to give me indigestion.' Chessie studied the food on her plate. 'Can we talk about something more interesting? Like why you work so hard?'

'I like working hard.' He frowned. 'Stop changing the subject and tell me about your father.'

'Only you can turn conversation into a series of orders. Why should I tell you?'

'Because you want me to understand you,' Rocco replied silkily, and had the satisfaction of seeing colour seep into her cheeks.

'True.' She gave a tiny shrug. 'Well, what exactly do you want to know?'

'Everything. Start with why your father didn't ever take you out, and then move on to why you think you're a useless artist when you're clearly extremely talented. And while you're at it you might as well cover the various ways in which he attacked your self-esteem.' He watched while she hesitated, and then put her fork down.

'Let's just say that my father and I weren't close,' she said quietly, reaching for her glass of water. 'You must have gathered that by now. He didn't want to spend time with me, but he had very strong views about my upbringing. He was very strict. Apart from school and during the olive-picking season, he didn't let me go out much.'

Rocco recalled the little he knew of Bruno Mendozo and decided that her story made sense. Certainly the older man had shown little respect or affection towards his daughter in public. 'But what about your teenage years? You must have gone out with friends?'

She picked up her fork and started to eat. 'He didn't allow it. I went to school. That was it. I did pretty well, but he didn't care about that because he didn't think education was important for a woman. He just wanted me to pick the olives and help behind the scenes in the office.'

Rocco sat back in his chair, his eyes narrowed. 'Are you trying to convince me that you meekly accepted the restrictions your father imposed on you? Because frankly, having seen you in action, I find it hard to believe that you didn't stand up to him.'

'I did.' Her gaze lifted, and her blue eyes were huge and shadowed. 'Just the once. Never again.'

There was something in her tone that sent a chill down Rocco's spine. 'What did he do?' His gaze burned into hers, demanding an answer, but she immediately looked away.

'It just didn't turn out to be a good idea, that's all. This fish is delicious.'

Deciding that a restaurant wasn't the most appropriate venue for in-depth questions about her childhood, Rocco moved on. 'So, if you didn't go out, how did you spend your time?'

'I drew. And I read.' She examined the piece of fish on her fork and then popped it into her mouth. 'I was an obsessive reader. In real life I've never travelled anywhere, but in my mind I've been everywhere. Take Florence, for example. I've visited the Duomo and the Baptistery. I've seen the frescoed chapel at the Palazzo Medici Riccardi. I've walked over the Ponte Vecchio and I've seen the statue of David. I'm very good at picturing things in my head.'

He found himself watching every movement of her face, noticing the way her mouth curved and her eyes gleamed with enthusiasm. 'You read about Florence?'

'At length. I lay in my bed, trying to imagine what it must have been like to live in Renaissance Florence. Then I read about Rome…' Her voice trailed on as she described with almost breathless enthusiasm, all the things that had interested her, and it was only when she finally stopped talking and blushed slightly that he realised he'd completely forgotten the existence of other people in the restaurant and had eaten a meal that he hadn't even tasted.

He glanced around him to find the other tables empty.

'I've been talking too much, but I just love it here.' She gazed down over the city. 'If there's a better view in the world than that then I certainly can't imagine it. It's the colours, I think, that make it so special. The red of the roofs and the buttery vanilla colour of the houses—it's as if someone stood up here and decided how the city should look as a whole.'

Rocco followed her gaze, trying to see the city through her eyes. 'Florence has been one of my homes for so long perhaps I don't see it properly any more,' he said softly. 'But I think perhaps it's time to do so again.' He shifted his gaze to the waiter, who gave a swift nod of understanding and produced the bill. 'Let's go, *angelo mio*. I have something to show you.'

He took her to all the sights, on foot, like the tourist she'd always wanted to be.

They wandered through narrow streets, making the most of the shade created by overhanging roofs, and occasionally forced to leap to safety to avoid being hit by one of the seemingly endless scooters that buzzed noisily around the city.

'Look up—' He caught her arm and pointed. 'This is one of the oldest parts of the city. That's a house tower. In the Middle Ages people used to fortify their homes so that they could defend themselves from attack.'

'Who attacked them?'

'Mostly the neighbours,' Rocco said dryly, pulling her further back onto the pavement as another scooter shot past with an apparent death wish. 'In medieval Florence everyone was always fighting with each other.'

Chessie laughed. 'So the hot Latin temperament hasn't changed much, then?'

They carried on walking, and it seemed to Chessie that every time they turned a corner they were given a different view of the famous red brick and white marble dome that formed part of the cathedral of Santa Maria del Fiore.

'I can't believe they managed to build something like this so long ago,' she breathed, as they finally walked into the Piazza del Duomo. Avoiding a chattering group of tourists, she stepped to one side and tilted her head back so that she could admire the sheer magnitude of the building.

'I suppose the Florentines were pretty impressed, too.' Rocco smiled at her, clearly amused by her fascination. 'Do you want to go inside?'

'Of course.' She glanced at him uncertainly. 'If that's all right? I don't suppose this is very interesting for you, is it? Seeing as you come here so often. Are you bored?'

He looked down at her for a moment, and a strange expression flickered across his handsome face. 'Not bored,' he assured her softly. 'Not bored at all.'

Chessie felt warmth touch her cheeks, and knew it was nothing to do with the sun. *No,* she told herself firmly. *She wasn't going to make the mistake of thinking that he cared about her.* She'd been there before, and it was a fast road to misery.

They enjoyed the cool silence of the cathedral, and then walked through the streets to the Foundling Hospital.

'It used to be an orphanage,' Rocco told her as he led her inside. 'There's a painting that I want to show you.'

They walked past a sleepy courtyard, up some stairs, and into a narrow gallery that overlooked another *piazza*.

The painting was at the far end of the room, and yet it dominated the space with the sheer vibrancy of its colour.

'I thought you'd like it,' Rocco said as he guided her towards it.

'It's beautiful.' She listened while he told her about the painting, and then they moved through the gallery and she paused by a smaller painting that caught her eye.

'How do you know so much about Renaissance art?' She

dragged her eyes away from the painting and tried not to think about the fact that any of those artists would have wept to be given the opportunity of recording the masculine perfection of Rocco's features. 'Did you go to university?'

He gave a faint smile. 'I have a degree in law from Cambridge and an MBA from Harvard, so the answer to your question is yes. But I'm afraid I didn't study art. My ambition at the time was to earn enough money to allow me to collect art. I have a number of pieces in the *palazzo* that will probably interest you.' He named a couple of paintings and her eyes widened.

'But those paintings are in a private collection. I've read about them.'

'Yes.' His tone was amused. 'They're in *my* private collection.'

'Oh.' For a moment she was silent, digesting the implications of that announcement. 'I never really saw the point of money before now, but being able to actually own something so beautiful and look at it every day whenever you like...' she breathed. 'You're extremely lucky.'

He laughed. 'Do I need to point out that you also own them? And certainly you can look whenever you wish. They're in the library on the second floor. Just don't touch, or you'll have the entire Florence police force descending on us.'

'Can I ask you something?' They walked out of the building and she lifted a hand to shield her eyes from the sudden glare of the sun. 'Did you buy them because you loved them, or because you thought they'd be a good investment?'

'Both,' he said instantly. 'Art is always a sound investment, but I refuse to have something on my walls that doesn't give me pleasure to look at. Your skills with a pencil are incredible. How are you in watercolours and oils?'

She blushed. 'I did a little at school, but not much. My father didn't encourage me to paint at home.'

'You should have gone to university. Studied.'

'That would have required a degree of freedom I was never allowed.' She walked down the steps into the *piazza* and wandered over to the fountain decorated with sea monsters. 'I went to the convent school in the village, but that was about the limit of his tolerance—and even that stretched it sometimes.'

'I can't believe your life was so restricted.' He slipped an arm round her waist and guided her past a group of tourists. 'What about your friends?'

'I didn't have any friends. I was tall and gawky and a completely different shape to all the other girls, and I was horribly shy. To be honest, I probably wasn't a very interesting person to be friends with.'

They left the *piazza* and walked up a narrow street. 'You're very open and honest, so I find that hard to believe.'

'Well, it's true. What about you? Tell me something about your childhood.'

She felt the instant change in him. Felt the tension in his body and saw the lines of his face harden. 'There's nothing to tell.'

'Of course there's something to tell!' She stopped and grabbed his arm, frustrated by his lack of response. 'According to the papers you made your first million when you were only nineteen.'

'I was seventeen, and it was four million,' he drawled, and she gave a little shrug and smiled.

'So why did you do it?'

He looked down at her and then gave a short laugh. 'Isn't that typical of you? Every other person I know would ask *how* I did it, trying to work out whether they had the skills to do it too. Only you would ask *why* I did it.'

'So?' Chessie prompted him, undaunted by the faint sarcasm in his tone. 'Why?'

'Doesn't everyone want money?'

'Enough money to live comfortably, of course. But you must have been driven to make that money at seventeen. And you're still driven. I'd like to understand why.'

'Well, you've just put your finger on one of the major differences between us. You want me to understand you, but I don't need you to understand me.'

'But I *want* to understand you,' she said breathlessly, struggling to keep up with his long stride.

'I like work.' He gave a dismissive shrug. 'I'm driven. End of story.'

Chessie frowned. It wasn't the end of the story, but it was obviously all he was prepared to tell her.

But there was time. Their relationship was still quite new, she reasoned. Perhaps he'd open up in time.

'I've always wanted to see the monastery at San Marco. Can we go?'

'Tomorrow.' He glanced at his watch. 'Walking round Florence can be exhausting, and you need a rest before tonight.'

'Why? What's happening tonight?'

'We're going to a nightclub.'

'You said you wouldn't ever take me to a nightclub,'

'That was before I discovered that you've never been to one.' He glared at her. 'Don't look so delighted. You're not dancing with anyone but me.'

'I wouldn't want to.' Chessie clapped her hands and on impulse stood on tiptoe to kiss his cheek. 'Thank you. That's the most romantic thing you've ever done.'

'Taking you to a nightclub is romantic?' He raised an

eyebrow. 'I filled your bedroom full of flowers. That was romantic.'

'No,' she said gently as she slipped her arm through his. 'Your *assistant* filled our bedroom full of flowers, so it wasn't romantic at all. But taking me to a nightclub because I've never been, even though it isn't what you want to do yourself. That's romantic.'

He studied her for a moment, his eyes narrowed. 'You're extremely complicated.'

'No, I'm very straightforward.' She hesitated. 'Will you help me find a job, Rocco?'

She felt his withdrawal. 'You don't need a job.'

'Not everything is about money, Rocco. I want to go out and work. Meet people.'

'By all means draw. I've already decided to have one of the upstairs rooms converted into a studio for you—it faces north, so the light is perfect. There is absolutely no reason for you to have a job.'

'Except that I want one.' She struggled to make him understand. 'I want to be independent.'

He looked at her with mounting exasperation. 'Millions of people out there dream of winning the lottery so that they can give up work, and you're telling me that, despite the fact that you are wealthier than people's most avaricious fantasies, you want a job?'

'That's right. It isn't about the money. It's about independence. I want to earn my *own* money and meet people.' For some reason this innocent statement seemed to increase his tension, and he sighed and stabbed his fingers into his hair.

'I'm beginning to understand just how restricted your life has been so far, and I'm prepared to let you do many things. But getting a job isn't one of them. There are people out there who aren't very nice, and thanks to your father you have absolutely no experience of life.'

'So you're going to keep me locked up?'

'Don't start that again. I'm taking you to a nightclub,' he reminded her. 'So I can hardly be accused of locking you up.'

'How many bodyguards will we have?'

'You'll have me,' he said grimly. 'And if anyone so much as glances at you they're going to find themselves in hospital.'

She stared at the hard lines of his handsome face and felt something flip inside her. *It would have been all too easy to believe that he cared about her.*

CHAPTER EIGHT

HE TOOK her to an exclusive nightclub and she danced until her body ached and her lungs threatened to burst.

Infected by the music and the electric atmosphere, Chessie discovered a sense of rhythm that she hadn't known she possessed, and she danced and swayed, aware that Rocco was showing no interest in anyone but her. As the dancing brought them close and then parted them again, their eyes met and the tension rose, sizzling to dangerous levels.

By the time they left the club something was alive between them, and the moment Rocco closed the bedroom door there was no longer any doubt about his intentions.

'I've been waiting to do this all night,' he groaned, taking her face in his hands and bringing his mouth down on hers. 'I'm not sure that going out with you in public is going to work for me. I'm rapidly discovering that my self-control isn't as impressive as I thought it was.'

And she suddenly discovered that she no longer cared about going out. All she wanted was to be with Rocco.

Her lips parted under the determined pressure of his, and she shivered with excitement as she felt the erotic skill of his kiss. *He always had this effect on her.* One kiss was all it took. Her head swam, her knees weakened and her stomach flipped.

And perhaps he knew how she was feeling, because he kept his mouth on hers while his hands moved to her back, and he was still kissing her as her dress slithered to the floor, leaving her standing in only her underwear.

'Rocco—' she gasped his name as excitement gripped her, and felt the warmth and strength of his hands as he moved her towards the bed.

He lifted his head just enough to speak, and his dark eyes were full of promise. 'You once asked me if I thought you were sexy,' he said huskily. 'I think you now have your answer. You're the sexiest woman I've ever seen.'

She pushed the jacket from his shoulders, driven by a feverish impatience to be closer to him. 'I thought you didn't want your wife to be sexy.'

'I was wrong about that.'

'Wrong, Rocco?' Despite the alarming rate of her heart, she still managed to tease him. 'I didn't think you were capable of being wrong.'

He gave a predatory smile, tipped her back on the bed and took his weight on his arms, so that he hovered over her. 'On this occasion I'll try and live with it,' he murmured, his own breathing quickening as she released the buttons of his shirt.

'Take it off,' she urged as she slid her hands over his chest. 'I want to see all of you.' The broad spread of hair over his pectorals narrowed at the base of his ribcage, drawing the eye downwards, towards temptation.

She reached for the belt of his trousers just as the shirt joined the jacket in a discarded heap on the floor.

'Not yet.' He pushed her back down onto the bed and slid his hands down her body. 'There's something I need to do—'

She felt him remove the wisp of silk that was the only thing covering her, and then gently push her thighs apart. A flicker of hesitation cut through her excitement as she realised his intention, and she felt the colour warm her cheeks as she felt the slow, deliberate stroke of his tongue touching her intimately.

She opened her mouth to tell him to stop, but all that emerged was a whimper of ecstasy as his mouth seduced her with an astonishing degree of expertise.

How could he know so much about her body? she wondered dimly as she shifted her hips against the sheets in an attempt to relieve the almost unbearable tension inside her. How did he know exactly how to touch her?

Just when she thought she couldn't bear the incredible sensations any longer, he moved back up her body, slid an arm underneath her and entered her with a decisive thrust that wiped every coherent thought from her head.

'*Dio*, you feel good,' he groaned, surging into her without restraint. His strength blended with her own burning heat, and the incredible intimacy drove the breath from her body. She felt the thickness of his arousal, felt the incredible sensations brought on by the skill and power of his thrust, and almost immediately exploded into an orgasm so intense that she gasped against his mouth, her nails digging into his back.

He slowed the pace, his movements more languorous but no less arousing and she felt the sensations build in her body with astonishing speed. Then she peaked again, her cry of disbelief smothered by the seductive pressure of his mouth.

Weakened and dazed, she lifted her hands to his chest. 'You have to stop—'

'Why?' he growled the word against her mouth. 'Why would I want to stop anything so fantastic?'

Looking up at him, she was enveloped in a sensuous haze. He looked dark and dangerous and incredibly sexy. 'Because I can't—'

'You can, *angelo mio*,' he drawled softly. 'As you're about to find out.' He shifted her position slightly and she gave a whimper of disbelief as she felt her body respond instantly to the change.

'Rocco, no—'

'Yes—' He increased the pace and she lifted her hips to meet the demands of his, her body exploding with sensations she was unable to resist.

This time when she exploded into orgasm it didn't end. It just went on and on, consuming and devouring her, until she heard Rocco mutter something against her mouth, felt his sudden tension and the explosive molten release of his own climax.

Only then did her body finally release her from its state of erotic suspension.

Breathless and weakened, Chessie lay under him, aware of slick male muscle, harsh breathing and the power of his physique. But despite his weight she didn't want him to move—*didn't want the moment to ever end*.

Finally he lifted his head and looked down at her. But he said nothing.

She could feel him inside her still, and the connection was deliciously intimate.

'I'm sorry.' His voice was gruff. 'I promised to use contraception and I'm afraid I didn't think of it.'

She hadn't thought of it either. And suddenly she realised that the reason she hadn't thought of it was because she hadn't cared. All she'd thought about was being with him. *She loved him.*

The sudden realisation exploded in her head, pushing all other thoughts aside, and she lay still, digesting the enormity of her discovery.

'You're upset about it. I can see that.' He rolled onto his back, taking her with him. 'I really am sorry. Whatever you may think, I did intend to protect you.'

She struggled to speak. 'I'm not upset.'

His hand gently stroked her back. 'Something's the matter. I can tell.'

She'd just discovered that she was in love. That was what was the matter.

But Rocco didn't do love. She knew that.

'I was just thinking about today,' she said finally, knowing that some explanation was necessary and unable to offer him the truth. 'It was incredible. The best day of my life. Thank you.' On impulse she lifted her head and kissed him gently. She saw a faint frown touch his eyebrows and saw him hesitate. *Would he say something affectionate?*

Chessie held herself still, waiting.

But he simply drew her closer and his eyes closed.

She wasn't going to let herself be disappointed, she told herself as she heard the rhythm of his breathing change, indicating that he was asleep. He'd shown that he cared about her and that was the main thing.

They stayed in Florence for another month. During that time Rocco managed to track down her mother.

'She's on a world cruise,' he said dryly, handing a number to Chessie. 'Are you sure you want to call her? It seems to me that she did very little to make your hideous childhood better.'

'She did what she could,' Chessie said softly, staring at the number. 'I've often thought that she probably only stayed with my father because of me. I'd like to speak to her. We weren't exactly close, but it feels like the right thing to do.'

So she rang and had a short conversation with her mother, who was obviously determined to enjoy her new-found freedom and her new life.

As Chessie was enjoying *her* new life, too.

From Florence, Rocco took her to Rome, Sienna, Venice and Verona. They stayed in palatial hotel rooms, always with Rocco's security team on hand. And they accompanied her on her many sightseeing trips when he was working, because Rocco refused to let her wander the streets alone.

One afternoon she returned early from a visit to Pompeii, feeling incredibly sick. *Too much sun*, she thought as she took the lift straight up to the Presidential Suite, trying to subdue the queasy feeling in her stomach.

Rocco was working in the living room—papers spread over the table, the phone hooked between his ear and his shoulder as he scribbled in the margin of a report.

'The advert isn't right,' he was saying in a gritty tone. 'Get them back in, and if they can't do a better job then fire them and get four more companies to pitch for the account.' He replaced the phone and then noticed her standing in the doorway. 'Are you all right? You look pale.'

'It's nothing. Too much sun and sightseeing, I expect.' She gave him a wan smile, intending to go through to the bedroom for a lie-down. But then a glossy picture of a couple in a restaurant caught her eye. 'What's that? Why are you looking so angry?'

'Not angry,' he assured her, stabbing his fingers through his hair and waving a hand at the documents. 'Frustrated. My team have given the olive oil account to what is supposedly the best advertising agency around, and they have come up with nothing original. A child with a marker pen could have done a more creative job.'

She picked up the glossy pictures. 'I don't know anything about advertising. What are these supposed to be?'

He gave a wry smile. 'The fact that you even have to ask says a great deal about the lack of success they're having,' he drawled in a weary tone. 'What you're holding is the advert they've designed to go into the print media—magazines and things,' he explained hastily, when he saw the blank look on her face. 'And these are storyboards, outlining their concept for a television advert. It's all wrong.'

She stared at the picture of the man and the woman dining in what was obviously an exclusive restaurant. 'What did you want?'

'I have no idea,' he said honestly. 'Which is why they were appointed. Normally I leave this sort of thing to the board of my Italian division, but I made the mistake of getting personally involved in the olive oil project. The problem is I know what I *don't* want. And I don't want anything they've so far presented me with.'

Chessie frowned down at the picture. 'Presumably they're trying to show that the product is exclusive by putting two people in a restaurant. But you just don't get the feel of Sicily from this, do you? This couple could be anywhere, and they could be eating anything. You wouldn't know it was anything to do with olive oil if it weren't for the bottle in the corner—' She broke off, suddenly aware that she was talking about a subject that was entirely unfamiliar to her.

'Don't stop.' His eyes narrowed thoughtfully. 'Go on.'

She coloured slightly. 'Well, I don't know anything about advertising, but a picture is supposed to tell a s-story,' she stammered, wishing she'd kept her mouth shut. 'This picture tells me that the couple are out and having a good time, but it doesn't say anything about the oil.'

'So what would *you* say about the oil? What would *you* put in the picture?'

Chessie gave an embarrassed shrug. 'I don't know. I—' *Oh, what the heck?* she thought to herself, reaching for a pen from the table and finding a blank sheet of paper. 'I suppose I'd try and link the picture to the origins of the oil itself. The heat, the smells, the feel of Sicily. That's why the oil is good. It's the real thing. I know because I've picked those olives. This picture they've done could be anywhere, but if I was designing a picture I'd put the couple in Sicily.' Her pen flew over the page as she did a rough sketch. 'People looking at the picture should feel as though they're there. It should get them to associate the oil with the wonders of Sicily…' Her voice tailed off and suddenly she felt mortified. 'Sorry. I've never drawn an advert or anything. I don't know what I'm talking about.'

'On the contrary. What you're saying makes perfect sense.' He took the picture from her and nodded decisively. 'It's good. You can present your ideas and they can use them.'

'You're joking!' Her eyes widened. 'They might hate them.'

'So what? I love them, and it's my money and my product they're trying to ruin.' He dropped the picture on the table and hauled her against him, moulding her against his powerful frame.

She tried not to be distracted. 'I don't know anything about advertising.'

'But you *do* know a great deal about art, and you have an incredible eye. Also you're not jaded from working on countless accounts of a similar nature. You wanted a job, *cara mia*. I'm prepared to give you one. You can oversee production of the ad campaign for the olive oil. I want you to approve what they do.'

She pushed against his hard frame, trying to ignore the rush of dark, dizzying pleasure that came just from being close to him. 'No one will listen to me. I don't have any credentials. I—'

'You need to have more confidence in your skills,' he

commanded, releasing her with a sexy smile and reaching for his phone. 'What you've drawn in two minutes with a standard-issue hotel pen is vastly superior to anything produced by the creative department of the agency to whom I'm currently paying a small fortune. But it's your decision. Do you want the job or not? Yes or no?' He held the phone in his hand, one brow raised in question, and she felt suddenly breathless.

Terror mingled with excitement. 'Yes—no—'

There was humour in his eyes. 'You were supposed to choose between the two options, but I'll make an executive decision and take your first answer.' He dialled a number and waited, his eyes thoughtful as he watched her. Then he instructed whoever was on the end of the phone to arrange for the agency to fly down the following day. When he replaced the receiver she swallowed hard, her stomach fluttering with nerves.

'What if I do it and it all goes wrong?'

'Then I fire you, *tesoro*,' Rocco drawled, dropping the phone into his pocket. 'But don't worry. I'll console you in the bedroom. You still look pale. Are you sure you're not over-doing the sightseeing?'

'It's incredibly hot today. I thought I'd sit on the terrace and sketch in the shade this afternoon. I could think about your advert. Do some more detailed sketches.'

He gave a wicked smile. 'Or maybe you should lie down in a dark room. My advert can wait.'

She woke the next morning relieved to find that the sickness had passed, but feeling nervous about the meeting with her advertising agency. Up until now her sketches had only ever been for her pleasure. No one else had ever seen them.

Anxious about the impression she'd make, she dressed

carefully and scooped her hair into what she hoped was a serious, businesslike style.

'You look incredibly sexy,' Rocco growled as he strolled into the bathroom to pick up his watch. 'Wear something different.'

Chessie checked her reflection and then glanced at him with exasperation. 'Rocco, the suit is grey and it's incredibly sober.'

'Then it's not the suit, it's you,' he breathed, running a hand over the back of his neck. 'Perhaps I was stupid to allow you to mastermind this campaign.'

Wondering why such a possessive statement didn't annoy her, Chessie sighed. 'Just because you find me attractive, it doesn't mean everyone else does too.'

His eyes darkened. 'Don't you believe it. It's a good job I'm going to be there with you.'

'Do I look all right—seriously?'

'Seriously?' He gave a faint smile. 'You look more than all right. In fact I'm thinking of firing you before you've started, just so that I can take you back to bed.'

A warm glow of happiness spread through her body. 'That's a very sexist remark.'

'You wanted me to find you sexy, *tesoro*,' he reminded her in a soft drawl. 'You're not in a position to complain.'

And she had no intention of complaining. She loved the fact that he found her sexy—*loved the fact that he was so obviously addicted to her body*.

She didn't need more from him, she told herself firmly as she finished her make-up and picked up the sketches she'd worked on the previous evening.

There was a flutter of nerves in her stomach as Rocco gently pushed her into the room. It seemed as though a huge number of people were seated round the large oval table, and the murmur of conversation ceased as she slid into a vacant seat, feeling hideously self-conscious.

This was ridiculous, she thought to herself. Why would they listen to her?

But the moment she produced the sketches she'd made, and outlined her thoughts on what the pictures could convey, the room fell silent. When she finally finished speaking there was a buzz of excitement from everyone round the table.

'It's brilliant. Evocative, and yet with the style and sophistication you'd want associated with a premium product.' The man Rocco had introduced as the managing director of the agency leaned forward to examine the pictures more closely. 'That's a great concept,' he said, admiration in his eyes as he looked at her. 'And those drawings are unbelievable. Who do you work for?'

'Me,' Rocco said immediately, his expression cold and forbidding. 'I want your team to work up her concept, Luca. Can you do it?'

'Of course.' The man nodded. 'We'll have something for you to see at the end of the week, and I'll send a team to Sicily to find a suitable location for the shoot. A beach restaurant or something.'

'Why not film at the villa?' Chessie suggested, and then carried on quickly as Rocco lifted an eyebrow in question. 'You wanted to show that it's exclusive, and what's more exclusive than a private villa with an infinity pool? Not only is the oil a taste of Sicily, but it's a taste of Sicily at its most exclusive.'

'The suggestion being that by using the oil they're gaining a slice of the lifestyle they covet? Aspirational…' Luca waved a hand at his team, who were frantically making notes. 'Yes, I love it. It's clever. Plenty of subliminal messages. We can work with that.'

Rocco's mouth tightened. 'I'm not wild about advertising my property on international television.'

'We'll find another property,' Luca said immediately. 'It's the principle that's important. Luxury. Leave it to us.'

As they left the room, Rocco slid an arm round her waist and urged her into the lift. 'Well, you wanted a job—and now it seems as though you have one. Have you any idea how much money I'm paying them for developing *your* concept?' As the lift door closed he lowered his mouth to hers. 'You were fantastic. You ought to demand a fee from me for your services.'

She slid her arms round his neck and smiled up at him, the adrenaline still whizzing round her body, still feeling on an incredible high. 'It was *fun*. I loved it. I'd do it for nothing.'

'We'll go back to Florence, and then you can use the studio I've built for you to finish your drawings,' he said as the lift doors opened into the suite. 'Unless you'd rather go back to Sicily?'

She hesitated. 'I don't hate Sicily any more,' she said quietly, wandering over to the windows and staring down the tumbling cliffs to the sea. 'Whenever you're ready to go back, I'll go with you.'

'Good.' His tone was dry. 'Because I have no intention of leaving you here. Where I go, you go. Especially as you now seem to be responsible for the future success of my olive oil exports.'

They returned to Florence, and she worked night and day for the next few weeks as the agency developed her ideas for the advertising campaign. And she loved it. She spent the day on the phone—sometimes to Luca, sometimes on a conference call with the creative director of the agency—and together they refined the drawings she'd given them and turned her basic ideas into a commercial campaign.

The only drawback was that she found it incredibly tiring. Frustrated that she had so little stamina, when Rocco was so fired-up and energetic, Chessie said nothing, but started taking a nap in the afternoons in order to give her the energy to be sociable during the evening. Even with the nap she found herself exhausted and ridiculously tearful, and she didn't understand her own reaction.

Finally her life was everything she'd ever wanted.

She was drawing and using her art, she travelled with Rocco, and she knew he had plans to take her to New York very soon. And, although Rocco hadn't actually said that he loved her, he was incredibly attentive and surprisingly caring for a guy who wasn't exactly in touch with his own emotions.

So why did she keep bursting into tears?

What was the matter with her?

What more did she want?

The weeks passed, and finally everything was ready. The shoot had been successfully completed and her role was finished. Now it was just up to Rocco's team to finalise distribution details.

With that in mind he flew to New York, but although he invited her to go with him she refused, too exhausted to contemplate such a long flight for such a short space of time.

He'd be back in two days, she reasoned. And in the meantime she could catch up on her sleep.

Her increasing tiredness was worrying her, and she made an appointment with a local doctor, determined to seek out the cause.

'I've never felt like this before,' she told him as she sat in his consulting room the following afternoon. 'I just have no energy.'

The doctor examined her, took some tests, and then called her back into the room to give her the results.

'You've been working hard, you say?'

'Yes. Is that why I'm so tired?'

'No.' The man adjusted his glasses and gave a faint smile. 'You're tired because you're pregnant, *signora*.'

'That isn't possible.' For a moment Chessie just stared at him. 'I can't be.'

'Why can't you be?' His voice was gentle. 'You are married, are you not?'

'Well, yes, but—' Chessie broke off, her mind racing. Rocco used protection, but there had been those few occasions at the beginning... 'But I had periods,' she muttered.

The man gave a sympathetic lift of his shoulders. 'Sometimes when your hormones are settling down it is still possible to bleed slightly. I have your test results in front of me. There's absolutely no doubt that you're pregnant. With your permission I'll send you to a friend of mine who practises in the clinic just across the street. He's a very well respected obstetrician and he'll do a scan this afternoon. That will help us calculate your dates. Have you put on weight?'

Pregnant? Chessie bit her lip and tried to concentrate on what he was saying. 'Not really. A bit, I suppose. But we've been eating out a lot.' She'd been visiting various restaurants with Rocco.

Pregnant?

She waited to feel disappointment. Waited to feel as though her brief taste of life had been snatched away from her. But instead she just felt a warm glow of satisfaction. Her baby. Rocco's baby. *Their* baby.

It wasn't what she'd planned, but now that it had happened she was ridiculously pleased. Suddenly she just wanted to smile and smile.

She was finally going to have a family of her own. And it

was going to be full of warmth and love. Nothing like her own childhood.

'You're sure?' she said the words breathlessly, anticipating Rocco's delight when she told him. She knew how much he wanted a son. 'You're really sure?'

'Absolutely. Wait while I give my colleague a call, and then you can have that scan.'

An hour later she lay on a couch, staring at a roomful of high-tech equipment.

Rocco was going to be so surprised, she thought, as she watched the doctor study the seemingly incomprehensible shapes on the screen. *So thrilled.* Wasn't this what he'd wanted all along?

Calculating that she must have become pregnant in those first few days, it came as no surprise to her when the doctor announced that she was at least four months pregnant.

That explained the tiredness and the sickness she'd felt when they'd been staying in Pompei.

The obstetrician scribbled something on her notes. 'You weren't planning to become pregnant yet?'

'No, but it doesn't matter,' she assured him hastily, as she sat up and adjusted her clothes. 'Rocco is dying to have a son.'

'Well, he's going to have to wait a little while to fulfil *that* ambition,' the doctor said with a gentle smile, handing her a photograph of the scan. 'It's very obvious from this that you're having a little girl. Congratulations.'

'A girl?' Chessie sat for a moment, staring at the black and white picture in her hand. 'You're sure about that?'

'Yes, I'm sure.' The doctor frowned. 'Is that a problem?'

Was it? 'No,' Chessie said quickly, aware that the doctor was looking at her closely. She slid off the couch and slipped her feet into her shoes. 'It isn't a problem.' Not to her. But to Rocco—

As she left the clinic to walk home the pleasure and excitement oozed out of her, and her mind was filled with a dark, anxious feeling of foreboding.

Rocco wouldn't mind, she told herself firmly. But no matter how much she tried to ignore it, the voice of warning grew louder and louder in her head.

He'd talked about having a big family, and he'd talked about having sons, but not once in their relationship had Rocco ever mentioned having a girl.

She'd done exactly what her mother had done to her father.

She'd produced a daughter when what he'd longed for was a son.

Dizziness swamped her and she stood still for a moment, waiting for her head to clear before she walked in a daze back to the *palazzo*.

It would never work, she thought miserably. How could it? She'd grown up with a father who had longed for a son. She had first-hand experience of how it felt to be completely unwanted.

How could she take that risk with Rocco?

She wasn't going to let that happen to her child.

Which left her with only one option.

CHAPTER NINE

SOMETHING was wrong.

In the car on his way from the airport, Rocco checked his watch for the fiftieth time and shifted impatiently in his seat as he attempted to contain his mounting frustration.

Thanks to a sudden crisis in one of his companies, he'd been forced to spend an extra day in New York, instead of returning to Florence as planned. Which shouldn't have been a problem.

But Chessie hadn't been her usual bouncy self on the phone the night before. It had been obvious that she had something on her mind.

He frowned slightly, acknowledging the flicker of worry that had been growing inside him since that phone call. Even though she'd obviously been trying to hide it, he hadn't missed the fact that she'd been unusually tired lately, and suddenly he felt cold fingers of panic stroke his spine.

Was there something wrong with her?

Something that she wasn't telling him?

Could she be ill?

No, surely not. She hadn't lost any weight. If anything her gorgeous curves were even more marked—but he put that down to all the evenings they were spending in restaurants. Chessie was a strong, healthy girl, and her tiredness was undoubtedly due to their extremely active sex-life. *Which meant that the problem lay somewhere else entirely.*

Examining the facts and sifting through the options, Rocco came up with another possible explanation. Could Chessie be in love with him and afraid to tell him?

He slid a finger inside the collar of his shirt, waiting for the usual alarm bells to ring. Of all the statements designed to kill a relationship in a single instant, he'd always found *I love you* to be the most deadly.

But somehow the thought of Chessie saying those words made him feel warmth instead of the usual panic.

And why not?

There was nothing wrong with her loving him. She was his wife. She was *supposed* to love him.

Tonight he'd encourage her to be honest about her feelings.

Suddenly he wished he hadn't stayed the extra night in New York. He should have been at home, getting to the bottom of the problem. Acknowledging his powerful need to see her again, Rocco was forced to face up to the uncomfortable truth that for the first time in his life he was missing a woman.

He missed Chessie.

But that really wasn't so surprising, he reassured himself hastily. They'd spent a great deal of time together lately, and she was entertaining company. She had a fresh, unspoilt quality about her that he found refreshing after the numerous socialites he'd dated in the past. And the dedication she'd shown towards the advertising campaign had delighted him. It was obvious from her minute attention to detail that she was a perfectionist, and possessed exactly the skill-set that he demanded from anyone employed in his organisation.

The only difference was that she wasn't an employee. She was his wife.

And no employee had ever affected his blood pressure the way his wife did. Never before had he disturbed his working day to indulge in hot, mindless sex, but he'd done exactly that with Chessie—and on more than one occasion.

By the time he strode into the *palazzo* a few hours later, he'd already planned how they were going to spend the evening. So he was surprised to see Chessie standing on the terrace, looking incredibly nervous.

Nervous?

He gave a faint frown as he discarded his jacket and loosened his tie. Why would she be nervous?

Was telling him that she loved him really that hard?

Chessie stood on the terrace and watched his approach.

He looked fabulous, she thought weakly, eyeing the iron-grey Italian suit and the arrogant tilt of his dark head. *Like a conqueror returning from success on the battlefield.* Had Rocco ever had doubts about anything? Was he ever unsure about anything?

She closed her eyes, took a deep breath, and put her hands behind her back to hide the fact that they were shaking.

She was doing the right thing, she told herself firmly. *The only thing.*

But everything would be so much easier if she didn't love him.

He paused in the doorway, and for a moment she thought she saw his normally cool, almost bored expression soften into something gentle. Wishful thinking, she told herself firmly, bracing herself as he strolled across the terrace and dropped a lingering kiss on her mouth. Rocco had been deprived of sex for three entire days. For a man of his libido, it was natural that any woman would be a welcome sight. It wasn't personal.

All the same, the reaction of her body was instantaneous, and she struggled to resist the temptation to collapse against him and let him do the rest.

It wasn't going to happen.

Instead she took a step back and waved a hand at the table. 'Do you want to eat straight away?'

He registered her deliberate attempt to put distance between them with a slight narrowing of his eyes. Then he lifted a hand and loosened his tie, his eyes flickering towards the table. 'You're hungry?'

He was obviously surprised that they weren't ripping each other's clothes off, and she could hardly blame him for that. Wasn't that what they'd done repeatedly for the past few months? Wasn't that what he expected?

'I'm not particularly hungry,' she said quickly, knowing that eating would be impossible for her. 'I just thought you might be. You've had a long journey.'

His eyes rested on her face, his gaze disturbingly sharp. 'I can see that something's wrong. Why don't you stop clenching your fists and biting your lip and just tell me? I've never been a lover of taut atmospheres.'

He constantly surprised her, she thought miserably. Just when she really, *really* needed to focus on his ruthless streak, he displayed an uncanny insight that came perilously close to sensitivity.

'I—' Her voice cracked, and she stopped and then tried again. 'I need to talk to you.' She might as well say it straight away. Why not? What was the point of waiting?

'Of course you do. That's entirely obvious.' He smiled

with his usual self-assurance. 'Just say whatever it is that's on your mind. Don't hold back.'

'It isn't that easy—'

'I believe in plain speaking,' he assured her, stepping forward and taking her hands in his. 'Whatever you tell me is fine. I'm listening.'

Her tummy did a somersault. 'I want a divorce.'

There was a taut silence, and then he released her hands and the indulgent look in his eyes changed to incredulity. 'Is this some sort of joke?'

'No. It's not a joke. I—this marriage isn't working for me, Rocco. I really do want a divorce.'

He took a step backwards, his hands spread in a gesture of disbelief. 'You are in my bed several times a day, and when we're not in bed we're naked in a different venue. Just which bit doesn't work for you?'

'That's just sex, Rocco. Marriage is supposed to be about more than sex.'

His eyes narrowed. 'Our marriage *is* about a great deal more than sex, and you know it.'

She did know it. But that knowledge did nothing to change her mind.

She *knew* she was doing the right thing, but telling him was proving even harder than she'd anticipated, and she was glad she'd spent the time thinking about her answer. 'It isn't really about us, Rocco. It's not even about you. It's about *me*. The person I've become. I just don't want to be married any more.'

His handsome face might have been chiselled from stone. 'Marriage isn't something you dip in and out of.'

'I know. That's why I don't just want a separation.' It was proving impossible to look at him. 'I want a divorce. I want to make it final.'

There was a long, throbbing silence, and then he paced the length of the terrace and stopped with his back to her, treating her to a daunting view of his broad shoulders. 'Why?'

Surely the fact that he wasn't looking at her should make it easier to speak the words she'd rehearsed? 'For the first time in my life I've been able to do the things I've always wanted to do. And I'm loving it. I want my freedom.' She almost choked on the words, and when he finally turned to face her his eyes were so cold that she shivered.

She felt what they'd shared slip away from them, and was suddenly enveloped by a desperate sense of loss and desolation. The usually warm, fragrant terrace seemed cold and inhospitable, as if a frost had descended in the middle of summer.

It was too late for them.

No matter what she said now, it was too late to mend the damage she'd done. She had to go forward. 'Is it really so surprising?' Her voice was a whisper, but it was the best she could manage. 'I've just discovered life, Rocco. There are so many things I want to do. I can't do them if I'm married.'

She waited for him to speak. To shout. To do or say *something*.

But he was completely silent, and his handsome face was an expressionless mask.

Everything twisted inside her, and suddenly she could hardly breathe.

She wasn't hurting him, she assured herself frantically. He didn't love her, so how could her words hurt anything except his ego?

'I'm going to fly back to Sicily in the morning and spend some time with my mother. I'll see a solicitor while I'm there.'

Speak, Rocco, she urged silently. *Say something. Anything.*

He stood for a moment without moving, then drew in a deep breath and walked past her without saying a word.

Battered by emotions that were entirely unfamiliar, Rocco stood in his study, struggling to make sense of the situation. But for the first time in his life his talent at problem-solving appeared to have eluded him.

Of all the things he'd anticipated that Chessie might want to tell him, *'I want a divorce'* hadn't been one of them—and her unexpected declaration had left him without a response.

She wanted a divorce.

Hadn't that been almost the first thing she'd said to him four and a half months ago, when he'd met her from the airport?

And hadn't he immediately denied her?

So what had changed? Why hadn't he been able to utter the same denial this evening, when she'd looked at him so expectantly, waiting for his response?

His hand gripped a brimming glass, and then he swore again and put it down on the table. Getting blind drunk, although appealing in the immediate term, wouldn't change the facts. And the facts were that he cared about her happiness.

At what point, he wondered with irony and no small amount of surprise, had her happiness become more important than his own? And what exactly did it mean when you were prepared to allow someone do the very thing that was designed to hurt you the most?

He'd always been arrogantly confident in his ability to understand women, but suddenly he found himself floundering.

He swore softly and tried to understand. She'd said that she didn't feel fulfilled, and yet how could that possibly be the case?

Up until he'd left for New York, she'd been happy. He had absolutely no doubt about that. There had been no talk about needing more freedom. No talk about leaving. And certainly no talk of divorce.

A frown touched his brows, and he abandoned thoughts of his drink and instead sprawled in the nearest chair, his long legs outstretched and his eyes narrowed as he sifted through the facts at his disposal.

All the facts suggested that something had happened while he was away.

But what?

What could possibly have caused such a catastrophic about turn on her part?

His mouth set in a grim line, he stood up and picked up the phone.

He had absolutely no idea what was going on, but he knew how to find out.

Chessie was sitting on the bed, gloomily contemplating her future, when Rocco walked into the bedroom.

The sun was already high in the sky, but it was obvious from his crumpled shirt and his darkly shadowed jaw that he hadn't been to bed. She felt something shift inside her, and struggled to control the almost excruciating love she felt for him. Even after a sleepless night he managed to look impossibly handsome, his shoulders broad and strong, his casual attire effortlessly stylish.

He was the sort of man who made a woman do stupid things.

But not her, Chessie reminded herself hastily. Not her. Not this time.

This time she was going to do the *right* thing—*for her child, if not for herself.*

'I was just about to start packing,' she muttered, and he came to a halt directly in front of her.

'Don't bother,' he responded in a cool tone, 'because you're not going anywhere.'

She closed her eyes. This was the response she'd expected the night before, but he'd been silent. Why now? Was it because he'd had time to think about her request? 'Rocco—'

'Tell me, *tesoro*,' he strolled towards her, his eyes fixed on her face. 'At what point did you intend to tell me that you are pregnant?'

She froze. 'I -'

'Lost for words, Chessie?' His beautiful mouth was set in a grim line. 'Finding it hard to tell me that I'm going to be a father?'

'How did you find out?'

'That isn't important. What *is* important is the fact that the person I should have heard it from was you. You *know* how much I want a son,' he said, his voice raw with pain, 'and yet even knowing that you were prepared to leave without telling me. *You asked me for a divorce.* Tell me, Francesca, is the prospect of motherhood really so distasteful to you that you'd keep your pregnancy secret? What were you planning to do? End it?'

'No!' Her eyes widened in horror and she flinched at the thought. 'How could you even *think* that? You know me better than that.'

'Obviously not.' His tone was hard. 'You were comfortable enough to seek a divorce without even informing me that you were expecting our child. Why would I not believe that you could be capable of terminating a pregnancy?'

Chessie placed her hand over her abdomen in an instinctive gesture of protection. 'Because I wouldn't do that.'

'Why?' His eyes were as cold as his voice. 'Why wouldn't you? You've spent the past four months telling me how much you want your freedom—how much you are enjoying your new life. Well, this really must have spoilt your fun.'

'It isn't like that.' She turned her head away, wishing that she'd left the night before. 'You don't understand. You have to let me go.'

'Let's get one thing straight, shall we?' His tone was solid steel. 'You're not going anywhere. Up until the moment I discovered that you were pregnant I was willing to sanction a divorce. But that's in the past. There will be no divorce. I am, however, willing to make some concessions to the fact that you're extremely unhappy with the situation. I'm willing to employ sufficient staff to ensure that you still have a reasonable amount of leisure time.'

Staff? Not comprehending, she gave a frown—and then her brow cleared. 'By "staff", you mean a nanny? I don't want that, Rocco. I want to look after the baby myself.'

There was a tight, tense silence while he raked her with an incredulous gaze. 'You are making absolutely no sense,' he growled, jabbing his fingers through his hair in a gesture of extreme frustration. 'You tell me that you want a divorce, but now you tell me you want to look after the baby.'

Chessie stared at the floor. 'You're right when you said that I didn't want a baby initially. I didn't. But when I discovered I was pregnant…' She rubbed her hand over her abdomen. 'I wasn't unhappy. I was thrilled.'

'Thrilled?' He hesitated over the word, as if he were translating it in his head and checking the meaning. Then he let out a long breath. 'Perhaps we should switch to Italian, because my understanding of this conversation is severely limited. If you were thrilled then why did you ask me for a divorce? Why are you leaving?'

She struggled to find her voice. 'Because it's the right thing to do.'

Although how doing the right thing could feel so wrong, she didn't understand. She was torn between her love for Rocco and her love for her unborn baby.

'How can leaving be the right thing to do?' His voice was hoarse and his eyes glittered with an almost feverish intensity. '*Why* would you even consider leaving when you're having my son?'

'Because I'm not having your son, Rocco.' Chessie swallowed hard, forcing herself to hold his gaze. 'I'm having your daughter.'

The words fell into the tense silence and Rocco just stared at her.

For a moment he didn't speak, and then she saw his eyes cloud with a variety of different emotions, none of which made any sense to her. 'My *daughter*?'

'Yes, your daughter.' The stunned look on his face said it all, and she turned away so that her sick disappointment wouldn't show on her face. 'A little girl.' She couldn't help smiling through the building tears. 'So now you understand why I'm leaving.'

'I understand *nothing*.' He caught her arm and turned her back to face him, his eyes burning into hers. 'Why does the fact that you are having a daughter change anything at all about this situation?'

'Do you really have to ask me that question?' The words almost choked her, and he studied her face for a long moment, as if trying to find the answers to his questions.

'This is about your father, isn't it?'

'It isn't about my father, no.' She pulled away from his grip, ignoring the dangerous edge to his tone. 'It's about us, Rocco. About *you*. About what you want and need.'

'You clearly know *nothing* about what I want and need.'

'You're a traditional Sicilian male. You want a son. You've been telling me that for the past four months.'

'Of course.' He dismissed her statement with an angry wave of a bronzed hand. 'But that doesn't mean I'm not equally happy with a daughter. You're making assumptions about me.'

'You always talk about having a son. You've never once mentioned a daughter.'

'It was just a figure of speech. An expression.' He sucked in a deep breath, obviously fighting for control. 'You really thought I wouldn't want the child because it's a girl?'

'You've never given me any cause to think differently.'

His anger bubbled over. 'I've spent four months trying to show you I'm nothing like your father,' he said in a driven tone, 'and you *know* that family is important to me. I've always made that clear.'

'But I don't know why,' she said quietly. 'You never tell me anything about yourself. I talk all the time, but you don't. I know nothing about your background or where you come from. I know nothing about why you feel the way you do about family. I know nothing about your own family.'

'That's because I have no family.' He spoke the words in a flat, emotionless voice, and then turned and muttered something under his breath. 'There's nothing to tell.'

'How can you have no family? Do you mean you're not in touch with them?'

'No, that isn't what I mean.' He lifted a hand and rubbed the tips of his fingers over his forehead, as if to ease a nagging pain. 'This isn't something I ever discuss. It isn't relevant to my life.' His hand dropped to his side and he paced over to the window, keeping his back to her.

'Don't walk away from me, Rocco!' She slid off the bed

and stared at his rigid shoulders. 'Don't walk away from this conversation.'

He turned, and the sunlight glinted on his dark hair. 'You want to hear about my family? All right, I'll tell you. But it isn't a happy story, so I hope you're not in a sensitive mood.' His mouth tightened. 'My father shot my mother. She was twenty-five years old and having an affair with someone. He was so beside himself that he'd killed the love of his life he turned the gun on himself. I was two years old at the time.'

For a moment Chessie was so stunned she couldn't move. 'Rocco—'

'I don't need sympathy.' He delivered the words as a warning. 'I'm prepared to give you the facts because you seem to think that hearing about my past is essential to the survival of our marriage, but I have no desire to dissect my feelings.'

'But you were so little—' Just imagining it made her heart twist.

'I survived.' His voice was flat. 'Isn't that what happens, Chessie? You of all people should understand that, because your life has clearly been no picnic up until this point. I'm even starting to understand why you left on our wedding day. People survive. They do whatever has to be done, and they rebuild their lives in the best way they can.'

'But you were two years old—' She choked on the words. 'Tell me what happened to you?'

'You insist on hearing the details?' His expression was cold. Hard. 'There was a massive scandal. That's what happened. I went to relatives, and then friends, but none of them wanted me because I was a constant reminder of my father's sins.' He gave a humourless laugh. 'And I had a fierce temper. I think they were a little afraid of me.'

She was surprised. 'But you're always in control of your temper.'

'That's right.' He gave a grim smile. 'I learned two things from my father. The first was that allowing emotion to cloud your judgement is an extremely bad thing, and the second was that falling in love makes a man behave in dangerous ways.' His eyes held hers and she felt her stomach flip.

'So you had short-term relationships with air-heads who couldn't possibly match your intellect, or interest you in any way other than physically, and you married a safe, uncomplicated girl who seemed perfectly suited to give you the family you wanted? The family you'd never had.'

'Amateur psychology, Chessie?' There was a gleam of humour in his eyes. 'I would never describe you as uncomplicated but, yes, in a way I suppose you're right. That was the plan.'

'And the olive oil business? Why did you want that?'

'Because, although my business is now spread all over the world, I've never forgotten my Sicilian roots. I suppose the olive oil business is a small part of who I am. My tribute to a family I never knew.'

'I wish you'd told me this a long time ago.'

'Why?' His voice was rough. 'What difference would it have made?'

'I don't know. At least I would have understood more about you. I thought your womanising made you like my father, but I can see that you were driven by something entirely different.' She gave a sigh and sank back down onto the bed. 'Families. They have so much to answer for, don't they? And the scars they leave are never on the surface, which makes them so much harder to heal.'

'I'm completely healed,' he drawled. 'You were the one

who insisted on exploring my pedigree, and that, if I may say so, is a typically female trait. As far as I'm concerned the past doesn't need to have an impact on the future.'

Chessie stared at the floor for a moment, struggling to speak the words that had to be said. 'You married the wrong girl, didn't you?' She lifted her head and gave a wan smile. 'You wanted a safe, uncomplicated wife, and that's what you should have had. When I first asked you for a divorce I told you then that you knew *nothing* about me, but you still refused to concede that our relationship was over. But last night was different, wasn't it? Last night when I told you it was over you didn't argue with me. Obviously you've finally realised that it's never going to work between us.'

She sensed the building emotion in his powerful frame.

'That isn't true.'

'You're just saying that because you've discovered I'm pregnant,' she said softly. 'But a baby isn't glue, Rocco. Boy or girl, a baby can't hold together a marriage that was never meant to stick.'

'It's true that I started out wanting a quiet, uncomplicated wife who would give me lots of children,' he answered in a raw tone. 'But that isn't what I want now.'

'What *do* you want now?' Hope struggled to the surface, but was instantly smothered by doubts and fears.

'You.' He closed his eyes briefly and muttered something under his breath. 'I want you, Chessie.'

Heart hammering, she dug her nails into her palms to stop herself from reaching for him. 'I'm not the person you thought I was. I'm not that safe, uncomplicated girl.'

'I don't want the safe, uncomplicated girl,' he said. 'I want the person you really are. That's the woman I want as my wife and the mother of my children.' He hesitated, and then gave a weary smile. 'That's the woman I love.'

'Rocco—' She couldn't finish her sentence, and he watched her for a long moment before he let out a long breath.

'I know that you don't love me, and I can't change that, but I'm prepared to bend over backwards to ensure that you can live the life you've always wanted to live.'

'But last night—' She shook her head slightly as she recalled his icy control. 'You didn't even argue with me when I said I wanted a divorce. Why would you do that if you love me?'

'Because I finally discovered that if you love someone enough you want them to be happy. And I finally discovered the true meaning of the word vulnerable.'

Chessie looked at him. Rocco? *Vulnerable?* He was the strongest man she'd ever met. 'You were willing to let me walk away?'

'Your happiness means everything to me, but now I know you're pregnant we have to find another way of giving you what you want while staying as a family.' He reached down and drew her gently to her feet, his movements lacking his usual self-assurance. 'I can't let you leave me. And I can't let you take my daughter.'

Struggling to speak, Chessie discovered the lump in her throat. 'My father never forgave my mother for giving him a daughter. I grew up knowing that he hated me.'

'There's one thing I've been wanting to ask you.' His voice was soft. 'At lunch that day in Florence, you mentioned a time when you stood up to your father. I want to know what happened.'

'It was a long time ago.'

'Tell me.'

'The school was having an art competition and I wanted

to enter.' Her voice shook slightly as she recounted the incident. 'I painted at night, when he thought I was asleep.'

'And what happened?'

'My father destroyed it.' Even now the memory was painful. 'I was devastated. I'd worked so hard on that painting, and I was really proud of it. I lost my temper with him and I shouted. Told him he was a tyrant and a bully. He was incandescent with rage. I'd never seen him so angry.'

'He shouted?'

'He hit me. And then he turned on my mother, blaming her for not doing a better job with my upbringing. Blaming her for not producing a son. After that I never stood up to him again. At first it just wasn't worth it, and over time it just became normal not to speak up.'

Rocco took her face in his hands. 'It's a good job he's dead,' he said thickly. 'Because if he wasn't then I think I might very possibly have killed him myself for what he did to you.'

'It's over now. But you can see why I didn't want to go to the funeral. And when you met me at the airport that day and told me that my mother had disappeared, I thought for one awful moment that—'

'That he'd killed her?'

'I was being ridiculous. My father was an extremely unpleasant man, but he wasn't a murderer.'

'As you say, it's over now. It's the past, and you should think only of the future. And your future is here. With me.' He stroked her hair away from her face. 'Will you stay even though you don't love me?'

'I can't really answer that question because I've no idea how I'd feel in those circumstances.' Happiness bubbled up inside her as she reached up and slid her arms round his neck. 'I *do* love you, Rocco. I've known that for a while. When I discovered I was pregnant I was so thrilled, and then they told me it was a girl and I was just terrified. I didn't know you well enough to understand your thoughts, and I certainly didn't imagine you loved me.'

'But you asked me for a divorce. All those things you said last night—' His fingers tightened in her hair. 'About wanting your freedom, about wanting to do things—'

'I was protecting our daughter. I was doing it for her. Because I thought leaving was the only option. I had no idea how you really felt until today.'

The hard lines of his face softened and he dropped a gentle kiss on her mouth. 'Already you are a lioness, and she isn't even born yet. Our daughter is a lucky girl.'

'No, I think *I'm* the lucky girl.' Chessie murmured the words against his mouth. 'Because you love me and that means everything. Love is all that matters.'

He kissed her and then lifted his head, his eyes fierce. 'I can't believe you love me too. Knowing that, I'm never letting you go again. For me it's for ever. No matter what happens. No matter what challenges we face. It's for ever.'

'I'm not a meek, compliant wife,' she warned, and he gave her one of his sexiest smiles.

'But you're the only wife I want, *tesoro*.'

HARLEQUIN *Presents*

I ♥ HARLEQUIN *Presents*

BROUGHT TO YOU BY FANS OF
HARLEQUIN PRESENTS.

We are its editors and authors
and biggest fans—and we'd
love to hear from YOU!

Subscribe today to our online blog at
www.iheartpresents.com

Mediterranean NIGHTS™

*Things are heating up
aboard Alexandra's Dream....*

Coming in March 2008

ISLAND HEAT

by

Sarah Mayberry

It's been eight years since Tory Sanderson found
out that Ben Cooper seduced her to win a bet...
and eight years since she got her revenge. Now
aboard *Alexandra's Dream* as a guest lecturer for
her cookbook, she is shocked to discover the
guest chef joining her is none other than Ben!
And when these two ex-lovers reunite, the heat
starts to climb...in and out of the kitchen!

*Available in March 2008
wherever books are sold.*

HARLEQUIN Presents

HP12707

What do you look for in a guy?

Charisma. Sex appeal. Confidence.
A body to die for. Looks that stand out from
the crowd. Well, look no further—in this
brand-new collection, available in April, you've
just found six guys with all this, and more!
And now that they've met the women in these
novels, there's one thing on everyone's mind....

Nights of Passion

One night is never enough!

The guys know what they want and how they're going
to get it! Don't miss any of these hot stories where
spicy romance and sizzling passion are guaranteed!

Look for these fantastic April titles!

THE TYCOON'S VIRGIN
by Susan Stephens

BEDDED FOR DIAMONDS
by Kelly Hunter

HIS FOR THE TAKING
by Julie Cohen

PURCHASED FOR PLEASURE
by Nicola Marsh

HIS MISTRESS BY ARRANGEMENT
by Natalie Anderson

HER BEDROOM SURRENDER
by Trish Wylie

www.eHarlequin.com

HPP0408

He's proud, passionate, primal—
dare she surrender to the sheikh?

Feel warm winds blowing through your hair and the
hot desert sun on your skin as you are transported to
exotic lands.... As the temperature rises, let yourself
be seduced by our sexy, irresistible sheikhs.

THE SHEIKH'S
CONVENIENT VIRGIN
by Trish Morey

Book # 2709

Sheikh Tajik needs a convenient bride,
and custom demands she must be pure....
Once Morgan Fielding arrives in Tajik's country,
he announces he will take her as his wife!

**If you love our men of the desert, look for more stories
in this enthralling miniseries coming soon—
only in Harlequin Presents!**

www.eHarlequin.com

HP12709

HAPPY
Valentine's Day
from Harlequin and Silhouette!

Special Treat!

Since you love books
as much as we do, we
would like to give you a
special Valentine's Day treat
of romantic and heartwarming reads.

Go to
www.HarlequinSpecialTreat.com
to receive your free online reads from us to you!

Plus there's even more, including fun romance
facts, upcoming news, games, e-cards and more!

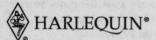 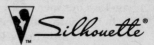

No purchase necessary.

VAL0208